Th[e Wilderness]

The Black Soul

Famine

Skerrett

'One of the most powerful novels that this master-writer has ever produced.'

The Irish Times

'Liam O'Flaherty is a great, great writer whose work must be unique in any language, any culture. He has all the potential for becoming a matrix for the yearnings of another generation.'

Neil Jordan

'Powerful in language, majestic in scope, utterly honest.'

Sunday Press

LIAM O'FLAHERTY

Born in 1896 on Inishmore, the largest of the Aran Islands, Liam O'Flaherty grew up in a world of awesome beauty, echoes from his descendants and the ancient pagan past. From his father, a Fenian, O'Flaherty inherited a rebellious streak; from his mother, a noted *seanchaí*, came the deep spiritualism and love of nature that has enraptured readers through the decades.

In France in 1917, O'Flaherty was severely shell-shocked. After a short recuperation, he spent several restless years travelling the globe. In 1920 he supported the Republican cause against the Free State government. Influenced by the Industrial Workers of the World's programme of social revolution, O'Flaherty organised the seizure and occupation of the Rotunda Theatre at the top of Dublin's O'Connell Street in 1922. He hoisted the red flag of revolution, calling himself the 'Chairman of the Council of the Unemployed', but fled three days later to avoid bloodshed. Later that year he moved to London, where his writing skills came to the attention of critic Edward Garnett, who recommended to Jonathan Cape the publication of O'Flaherty's first novel. For the next two decades, O'Flaherty's creative output was astonishing. Writing in English and Irish, he produced novels, memoirs and short stories by the dozen. Remarkable for their literary value and entertainment, O'Flaherty's books are also crucial from an anthropological point of view, charting the ways and beliefs of a peasant world before it was eclipsed by modernity.

Some of O'Flaherty's work was banned in Ireland — he was a rebel in his writing, as in his life. Liam O'Flaherty died in Dublin in 1984, aged 88 years, having enriched forever Irish literature and culture.

LIAM O'FLAHERTY
return of the brute

WOLFHOUND PRESS
& in the US and Canada
The Irish American Book Company

This edition published in 1998 by
Wolfhound Press Ltd
68 Mountjoy Square
Dublin 1, Ireland
Tel: (353-1) 874 0354
Fax: (353-1) 872 0207

Published in the US and Canada by
The Irish American Book Company
6309 Monarch Park Place
Niwot, Colorado 80503
USA
Tel: (303) 652-2710
Fax: (303) 652-2689

Wolfhound Press receives financial assistance from the Arts Council/
An Chomhairle Ealaíon, Dublin.

British Library Cataloguing in Publication Data
A catalogue record for this book is available from the British Library.

ISBN 0-86327-628-8

10 9 8 7 6 5 4 3 2 1

Cover Photograph: Imperial War Museum
Cover Design: Slick Fish Design
Typesetting: Wolfhound Press
Printed and bound by The Guernsey Press Co. Ltd, Guernsey, Channel
Islands

Chapter One

'Hey! What's that? D'ye hear something crawling along the ground to the right there?'

Gunn got to his feet and looked over the parapet. He peered into the darkness. Then he turned his head to one side and listened. There was no sound but the droning of the rain, falling on the sodden, naked earth of the battle front.

'I can hear nothing,' he said. 'Probably it was a rat you heard.'

He yawned and added:

'God! Is this rain never going to stop? There's eight inches of water at the bottom of this post already.

Oh! Oh! Oh !

This is a lovely war.

If I ever have a son I'll bring him up in petticoats.'

He had been dozing on the fire-step, when Lamont, the sentry, kicked him. Now, as he awoke fully, he began to shudder with cold. He rubbed his eyes and cursed. Then he noticed that Lamont, who leaned over the parapet beside him, was trembling violently.

'What's the matter, towny?' he said tenderly. 'Cold?'

Lamont did not answer. He trembled still more violently. Instinctively, he moved his body closer to Gunn. Gunn put his arm around the youth's shoulder and shook him.

'Hey!' he said gruffly. 'Come on, Louis. What's the matter? Got the wind up? Cripes! I can't see my hand.'

He held out his hand in front of his face and peered at it.

'I'm all right,' whispered Lamont in a trembling voice. 'It's only that bloke crawling about ... out there ... that ...'

'Oh! To hell with him!' said Gunn, taking away the hand that lay on Lamont's shoulder and inserting it in his left armpit, beneath his greatcoat, in order to scratch himself. 'There's nobody out there. It's only a rat. You sit down and have a draw at a fag. I'll stand here. Come on. Get out of it. God bless the man who invented fags anyway. Oh! Christ! I'm sleepy. If my mother saw me now she'd take to drink. Phew! I must have water on the brain. I'm soaked to the marrow. Step down, lad, and light up. I'll have a draw after you.'

Lamont got down hurriedly, crouched against the base of the parapet, took off his steel helmet and rummaged within the band until he found a packet of Woodbines. He took one from the packet and hurriedly put on his hat. Rain had begun to fall on his shorn skull, making it feel terribly cold.

'Poor little bastard!' muttered Gunn, now scratching himself with both hands. 'It's tough on a youngster. Christ! What a life!'

He shook his fist at No Man's Land and growled:

'Come on, you devil! Do your best. You won't do me in.'

Chapter One

They were in the outpost occupied by the bombing section of No. 2 Platoon. They had been in the line for forty-eight hours and it had rained ceaselessly all that time. There was no dug-out, except an elephant frame which covered the Corporal's corner. Eight of them had to sleep in the water that covered the bottom of the hole. It was impossible to drum up. Everybody was exhausted and demoralised; especially young Lamont, who was unused to the trenches and was only a youth of nineteen.

'Say, Bill,' whispered Lamont from the bottom of the hole. 'I can't light this fag. My hands are numb.'

Gunn stepped down.

'Give it to me,' he said.

Sheltering his head under Lamont's oil-sheet, he took the cigarette and the box of matches.

'Cigarette is wet now,' he said. 'So are the matches. Blast it!'

It took him a long time to light the cigarette. He puffed at it three times and then stood up.

'Here,' he said, 'have a draw. Do ye good. Blast this rain!'

He leaned over the parapet and began again to scratch himself.

'Say, Louis,' he whispered, 'are they biting you?'

'No,' said Lamont, smoking eagerly. 'At least, I don't notice.'

'You'd notice if they were,' said Gunn. 'Always worse when you wake up. That bloody creosote I put on my shirt only made them worse. Hello! That's not a rat.'

He heard a sound in front; obviously a man crawling about in the mud, dragging his body along the ground, or hauling something heavy. Lamont also heard the sound and jumped to his feet.

'There it is again,' he whispered excitedly. 'Do you hear it?'

'Sit down,' said Gunn. 'I hear it all right. It's probably that sniper we were talking to yesterday evening. He's all right.'

'I don't think so,' said Lamont nervously. 'They might be creeping up on us to capture us by surprise.'

'Well! What about it if they capture us?' said Gunn. 'We couldn't be worse off as prisoners.'

'But they might kill us.'

'Oh! Shut up, for God's sake!'

'The Corporal said this post was in a dangerous position, stuck out in front of the line.'

'You'll drive me mad,' said Gunn. 'Can't you learn how to soldier? As long as that sniping post is there within one hundred yards of us, they can't shell us. See? Anyway ... They're just as fed up as we are. It is only somebody coming to relieve that sniper. There you are. Listen. Hear them whispering?'

They listened. Above the droning of the rain, they heard voices muttering in the darkness. The voices did not seem human to them, as the words, uttered in a strange language, had no meaning in their ears. They appeared to be sounds uttered by animals.

'Hear them?' said Gunn. 'Funny, isn't it, hearing these two blokes muttering out there in their queer lingo. A Mills' bomb'd give those blokes a queer fright now, I bet. Still, he wasn't a bad little fellow, that sniper we were talking to yesterday evening. The bloody big lump of chocolate he gave us for two Woodbines. Old Reilly made him eat a bit before we swopped. It might be poisoned, he said. "You no fire, I no fire," said the bloody little Jerry. Funny little bloke with a ginger moustache. I've seen lots of Jerries in the States before the war. Great bloody beer sharks. Good-natured blokes. They're just driven to it, same as we are. Still, I'd like to drop a bomb on top of those two out there.'

Lamont shuddered. They listened in silence again to the muttering.

'Shouldn't we call the Corporal all the same?' said Lamont. 'It might be ... they might be ... it might be an attack.'

'He'll give you hell if you wake him,' said Gunn. 'Hear him snore?'

The two enemy soldiers stopped chattering and began to move away.

'What did I tell you?' said Gunn. 'See? They're moving off.'

They listened to the queer, brutal sound of two human bodies dragging themselves over the sodden mud in the darkness.

'It's funny,' said Lamont, 'those two blokes are soldiers same as we are, with people at home. And they're wet and lousy and hungry and fed-up same as we are too. But we think ... I mean to say that whenever I think of Fritz I see him only as some cruel giant that's ... No! But just as an enemy. What's an enemy, I wonder? It's something ...'

'Jesus!' said Gunn. 'You're only a kid. You have funny notions. You go and have a sleep. I'll stand here for you.'

'I can't sleep,' said Lamont. 'I'd rather stand here and

talk to you, if you don't mind.'

Gunn cursed and said:

'You put the wind up me. Strike me bloody stiff but you do. You can't stand this racket and you shouldn't be here.'

'Here,' said Lamont, 'have the rest of this fag.'

Gunn took the cigarette. He lowered his head as he drew at it, lest the glow might be seen.

'It's queer,' said Lamont, 'how a fellow never gets anything wrong with him in the trenches. I've been soaked to the skin for two days and I've slept in water. Still ... I haven't got a cold. At home, if I got wet like this I'd catch pneumonia. I wish I could get pneumonia. I'd get as far as the base anyway.'

'Shut up, for God's sake!' muttered Gunn, drawing eagerly at the butt of his cigarette. 'No use talking like that. Probably be dead before you got to the dressing station. Put that idea out of your head. You've got to stick it, mate.'

He threw down the butt of his cigarette. It sizzled in the water.

'You've been wounded twice, haven't you, Bill?' said Lamont.

'Yes.'

'What's it like?'

'How do you mean? Hospital?'

'No. What's it like getting hit? Does it hurt much?'

'How do I know? I don't remember. It hurt like hell at the dressing station. Quit talking about it. You'd drive anybody into a funk. You're like a woman. Can't you sit down and have a sleep?'

'No. I don't want to sleep.'

Gunn spat, cursed, rummaged in his clothes under his gas mask, grunted, pulled his hand and cracked a louse against the butt of his rifle.

'I'm crawling with them,' he said, shuddering. 'It's in the blood. The longer you're out here the worse you get.'

'Is there no way of getting out of here?' said Lamont.

'There's only two ways,' said Gunn angrily. 'You either go West or get a blighty. Now quit it or I'll give you a crack on the jaw. You'll drive me mad. I've got enough of a job looking after myself without looking after you. You're always nagging like a woman. Blimme! Can't you be cheerful sometimes?'

Lamont sat down on the fire-step. He got up almost at once, clutched Gunn's arm and whispered excitedly:

'Say, Bill, I can't stick this any longer. I'll go mad. Can't you get me out of it?'

Gunn gripped the lad with both hands and shook him.

'What are you driving at?' he said. 'Eh?'

'You could do me a good turn if you wanted to,' whispered Lamont.

'How d'ye mean? I can't get myself out of it.'

'Give me a blighty one.'

'What?'

'Lots have done it, haven't they?'

'That's enough now,' whispered Gunn, in a voice that was both angry and panic-stricken. 'Pull yourself together. You're a fine mucking-in chum to have. By God!'

Lamont dropped his face on his arms, against the muddy sandbags of the parapet. Gunn took him roughly in his arms and muttered:

'Listen. I know what's the matter with you. I'm going to give you a good punch in the jaw if you're not careful. You're just nagging like a woman. Chuck it.'

'Let me alone,' said Lamont, in a broken whisper. 'Only for mother, I'd do myself in. They'd tell her.'

'You'll do no such thing,' said Gunn. 'I'll see to that. I've no mother, but at your age I could stick this on my own legs, without no mother. Aye! And a double ration of it, boy. Damn this rain! That's the cause of it. Rain. Mud. Lice. Curse it!'

He looked up at the sky and clenched his fist, as if threatening heaven.

He was a huge fellow, so burly that he looked stocky, although he was well over six feet in height. He looked a typical fighter, with a thick neck, square jaws and a body like a full sack. His right ear was battered. There was a scar on his left cheek. He was thirty-two years old and he had laboured for wages since his boyhood, but his body had not become demoralised by enslaved toil. Nature had taken great pains with this seemingly crude and large individual, endowing him with muscles and sinews that refused to be stiffened by monotonous labour, and with a spirit that hardship could not conquer. He had a simple soul, which shone through his great, blue eyes; giving the lie to the cruel strength of his neck, his jaws, his heavy-lipped mouth, his massive shoulders, chest and thighs.

He was like a mastiff, that most ferocious-looking and most gentle of all animals; who, however, when roused or made vicious by brutal treatment, becomes as ferocious as he looks.

14

He looked down at Lamont and said, 'You'll drive me daft. I'm blowed if I know why I muck in with you. Strike me stiff, if I do. You're like a woman.'

Then he shuddered and looked into the darkness.

'You've been out here now,' he said, 'for three months. You should be getting used to it by now. But you're not.'

'I can't help it,' whispered the youth, 'I'm all in.'

Gunn shuddered again and struck himself a violent blow on the chest. Then he cursed and said with extraordinary anger:

'Now listen to me. I've been out here for over two years on this lousy front and I'm as fed up with it as you are. I don't give a curse who wins this rotten war and I'd like to run my bayonet through the fellahs that started it. We're just fighting for a gang of robbers, as '79 Duncan said. I've got my eyes open now, although I hadn't when I enlisted. I came thousands of bloody miles to enlist. Jumped freight all the way from Seattle, Washington, to New York, and then to Liverpool as a trimmer on a liner. See? I walked into it. But if I ever get desperate, same as you are, I'm not going to try and get out of it by wounding myself or running across No Man's Land to bloomin' Fritz with my hands up.'

He spat and added:

'That's a coward's way out of it. I promised to soldier and soldier I will, though I hate their guts, from the lousiest Lance-Jack to the Skipper.'

He spat again, cursed, looked at Lamont and said almost nervously:

'Jesus! You put the wind up me. I was married once to a woman, way up in Nova Scotia, when I was working on

15

a weekly boat. She was just like you. She had me worn to a ghost. I left her, by Jesus, one night, after giving her a bloody good hiding. I went out west and never saw her again.'

He peered down into the post, towards the corner where Corporal Williams lay asleep under an elephant frame. The Corporal was just a dun blur, from which sounds of snoring came. The dim forms of his comrades lay tossing in their sleep at the bottom of the hole, some of them with their feet in muddy water. Gunn tipped Lamont and whispered, jerking his head towards the Corporal:

'If he heard what you said, d'ye know what you'd get? Eh?'

Lamont shuddered, wiped his face with his sleeve and said:

'I don't care. They can put me up before the firing squad whenever they like. I'm fed up.'

Gunn ground his teeth.

'Then what the hell did you enlist in this mob for?' he said. 'This is the worst regiment in the whole army. Ye knew that. It's the best regiment, too! For I've seen our fellahs, by God, go through worse than hell. They're gathered from all corners of the earth, the toughest of the tough. You should have joined the Army Medical Corps.'

'I wish I had no mother,' whimpered Lamont.

'I can't stand this,' growled Gunn to himself. 'As sure as hell I'm going to get into trouble over this kid.'

Lamont had joined the battalion three months previously at a rest camp. When they saw him, the tough soldiers greeted him with jeering laughter. He was a beautiful boy, with pink cheeks, dazzling white teeth like a girl and big blue eyes. He did not swear or drink and it was obvious at once that he had never been used to any hardship. Almost as soon as he arrived he began to receive parcels of food and cigarettes with every post. It became known that his people were well-to-do and that he had a mother who doted on him and that he was an only child.

Gunn took him under his protection and cared for him like a father or a big brother. At first it made Gunn very happy. There had been no gentle influence like this in his rough and nomad life. He almost shed tears when he got a letter from Lamont's mother thanking him for being kind to her boy. 'God will bless you for it. He is the light of my eyes. My heart would break if anything happened to my darling boy.' Gunn had also reached the age when a virile man, who has no children, begins to look upon youth with longing; when the fear of death and old age begins to conquer the arrogant confidence of youth.

But after a while he became aware that the boy was sapping his strength. The boy lived on his nerves. Not only did he have to do the boy's work, but he had to comfort him, to lend him courage.

And now the boy's cowardice was sapping his sense of discipline; that extraordinary religion of the soldier which is proof against the greatest tortures; something that is brutally beautiful.

'Listen' he said, 'that's the worst act of cowardice a soldier can commit. And what's more, you can't get away with it. If a man could do that without feeling ashamed of himself, d'ye think there'd be a man left on this front? But, ye see, them blokes back there are too cute.' He nodded his head to the rear. 'You can't beat them.' He touched his forehead. 'Up there they've got it. Brains! We're mugs. Look at it that way. Supposing it wasn't a cowardly thing to give yourself a blighty one? Let's say you do it and get back the line. What happens? They'll cop you. Sure as hell. They've got blokes hired specially for copping self-inflicted wounds. They've got smart at it now. At first, you could get into hospital by eating a bar of soap. Now, if you try on any silly stunt, they put you in dock till you get better and then you're for it. I know. I've been out here nearly two years and I've seen many a man, good men too, chancing their arms. Thirty-Nine Townshend tried to wound himself in the head when we were in the straw trenches. The blighter blew his brains out by mistake. Eighty-Four Flynn broke his leg with an entrenching tool at Neuve Chapelle. They copped him. Ginger Moriarty was caught by an officer trying to wound himself in the thigh with his rifle. He got what was coming to him all right. Christ! They've got an hospital away back there for self-inflicted wounds. There's nothing to it.'

He dug his fist into Lamont's back and said:

'Savvy?'

'I'll get out of it somehow,' said Lamont with strange coolness.

Gunn peered at him in the darkness, almost with terror. A stupid fellow, the youth's curious feminine cunning unnerved him, and made him also feel the temptation to do something shameful and desperate. The youth's obstinate determination to save himself from the horrible life of the trenches roused in Gunn a dangerous desire for freedom. This desire was dangerous for Gunn because he was a brave soldier, who knew there was no means of escape, other than death or disablement inflicted by the enemy.

Terrified by the temptation inspired by the boy's words and manner, he instinctively glanced again towards the corner where the Corporal snored.

'Quit that!' he whispered savagely, turning back to Lamont. 'What are ye driving at now? Desertion? 'Fifty-Seven Flood tried that at Armentières. What happened to him? Caught on the wires and riddled with bullets. Disgraced his bloody company. Jerry'd make ye sorry ye came if ye got there. He doesn't want his own men trying that on, so he'd make an example of ye.'

'I'll get out of it somehow,' said Lamont coldly.

'God Almighty!' muttered Gunn.

They became silent, standing side by side, looking out into the darkness over the parapet. With their steel hats and their oil-sheets, which they wore, laced about their throats, over their greatcoats, they looked like ghouls in the gloom, buried to their waists in a hole; while all round them the earth lay naked, turned into mud, holed, covered with the horrid débris of war, emitting a stench of rotting, unburied corpses.

From the pitch-dark sky the rain fell, unceasing and monotonous, like the droning of brine water falling on a floor of black rocks from the roof of a subterranean cave where moaning seals are hidden and flap about up on their ledges; sounds from a dead world; the mysterious gloom of the primeval earth, where no life had yet arisen;

no sap of growing things; nothing but worms and rats feeding on death.

Clods of dislodged mud slipped from the sides of holes, flopped into blood-stained pools, sank and turned into slime.

The silence was horrid.

Chapter Two

Suddenly there was a loud crash in front. Lamont immediately ducked his head.

'What's that?' he whispered.

Another crash followed, a belching sound, preceded by a fountain of fire that rose, widening into an arch, with great swiftness and vanished in an instant. There was a series of crashes. When the sound of the last explosion died away, there was silence for a little while. Then a machine-gun began to cackle some distance to the right. That made a vicious sound; a snake's hissing magnified.

'That's one of ours,' said Gunn, looking to the right. 'Something must be happening. There were orders not to fire unless ...'

He ducked as a shell came whizzing over the post from the rear and, dropping short, burst ten yards in front of the post with a deafening roar. Immediately the men awakened from their sleep. They tossed about, instinctively making a movement to stand up and with the same instinct crouching for shelter when they realised that a shell had dropped near.

'Hey! What's that?' came the Corporal's voice from under the elephant frame.

Gunn opened his mouth to say something to the Corporal, but closed his mouth without speaking and sheltered his head quickly. An enemy machine-gun raked the post from end to end. Its sound was guttural, as if hoarse with fury.

Again the explosives boomed, now farther away, seemingly heavier, their harshness dulled by distance.

Gunn crawled stooping through the post to the Corporal. The Corporal was trying to crawl out of his shelter over two men who lay in the doorway, and who cursed one another, helplessly trying to disentangle their equipment.

'I think he's blowing up his front line, Corporal,' said Gunn. 'We've opened fire on the right.'

'Eh?' said the Corporal. 'What dropped there in front?'

'One of ours,' said Gunn. 'It fell short.'

'Fred Karno's bloody artillery,' said the Corporal. 'Stand to, everybody.'

Gunn crawled back, seized his rifle and got ready to open fire.

'Stand to,' cried the Corporal, kicking at a man who was trying to put on his gas mask. 'What are you doing?'

He pawed at the man.

'I'm taking no chances,' said a querulous voice.

'Who gave orders for gas masks?' said the Corporal.

'I'm taking no chances,' answered the voice.

'Get your blasted rifle and stand to,' said the Corporal. 'Jump to it, everybody. Heads!'

The enemy machine-gun was now rattling on the elephant frame.

'They've opened fire on us, Corporal,' cried a voice, dazed with sleep.

'What d'ye think I am?' cried the Corporal. 'Deaf and dumb?'

Two enemy shells dropped behind the post, the sound of their explosion almost smothered by the sodden mud, which they sent in a shower of heavy lumps into the air. The men, now fully awake and on their feet, gripping their rifles and bombs, began to chatter.

'Come on. Get out of my way. He's coming.'

'Move, blast it. Give me room. Let go my rifle.'

'Who? Fritz? Is he coming over?'

'Jesus! We're surrounded.'

Now there was a heavy artillery and machine-gunfire. The flashes of the guns, belching their shots, and of the shells, bursting, lightened the darkness in spots, making it still more awesome.

Awakened suddenly from sleep, they were dumb-founded by this sudden and dangerous activity in which they took no part. They had been lying out for two days in a hole without hearing a shot. Now, without warning, a thunderstorm had burst over their heads. They tried to crowd the parapet, but the post was so small that there was no room for them all. There was no order. Everybody was talking.

Gunn, although he had been awake when the fighting began, was as excited as the others. To him this sudden alarm was merely an ordinary incident in his trench life, but he had been disturbed by Lamont's seductive coward-ice and by the demoralising desire for escape born of Lamont's determination 'to get out of it somehow'.

Further, there had recently been continual rumours that the war was nearly over, that the enemy was retiring, that peace had, in fact, been already made. These rumours had, of course, been current since the first day that Gunn arrived in France; but of late they had been more persistent. All winter they had held that sector in practical idleness, as far as fighting was concerned. More exhausted and demoralised by the mud, hunger, rain, cold and constant 'fatigues' than they would have been by dangerous activity, they were quite ready to believe anything.

Now Gunn was thinking as he heard the shells burst: 'Suppose the war is over and I get killed by the last shell?'

Then he remembered Lamont and started, ashamed because he had forgotten the boy for a few minutes in his excitement. He stooped, looked and found that Lamont had buried his head into the side of the parapet and was lying as still as a rabbit which a dog has sighted. Gunn prodded him in the ribs and whispered in his ear: 'Stand to. Get your rifle.'

Lamont shuddered and tried to press his body still farther into the parapet. Gunn pulled him back, shook him and made him stand up. Almost at once he dragged him down and laid his body close against the bottom of the hole.

An enemy shell had landed right on top of the parapet, a few feet to the left of Gunn. It had come with that sharp screech which denotes an almost direct hit to the horror-stricken listener; the screech lasts just the fraction of a second of actual time, but it seems an eternity.

As the roar died away, swallowed by a more distant

roar, lumps of mud and pieces of torn sandbags began to fall. Then the top of the parapet gave way and flopped into the trench. Somebody groaned. Others cursed. There was a horrible stench.

Then there was silence. As if it had effected its purpose, the firing shifted to the right.

'God!' cried a voice. 'What's this lying on top of me?'

'Eh?' said the Corporal. 'Come on. Rebuild this parapet. Anybody hit? I heard somebody groaning.'

Nobody answered him. Everybody began to examine his own body. Then the first voice cried out again in horror:

'See? It's a dead man's leg. Blimme! One of them blasted Froggies that's buried here.'

'Whew!' cried another. 'I just stuck my hand into somebody's rotten guts. God! What a stink!'

There were guffaws of nervous laughter. Delighted that they had not been hit by the shells and that no more shells were falling near, they laughed; grateful for their spared lives and eager to prove their contempt for danger.

'Don't mind the stink,' said the Corporal. 'Build it up again. Throw all them Frenchmen out. Build it up. Anybody hurt, I say? Who's that moaning?'

Gunn was holding Lamont in his arms, shielding him from the Corporal. The bursting of the shell had thrown Lamont into a panic.

'I don't hear anybody moaning,' said Gunn.

He felt an extraordinary fear lest the Corporal might become aware of Lamont's cowardice; because he associated Lamont's cowardice with himself. He felt that it was getting a grip on him.

'Yer a liar,' said the Corporal.

Gunn punched Lamont under the chin. The youth stopped moaning.

'Well! Anybody'd groan if two sandbags fell on his head,' said Gunn. 'I got an awful wallop.'

'You're always getting in the way,' growled the Corporal. 'Why didn't you say so? Build up the parapet.'

The Corporal stood up in the hole.

'Listen,' he said in a gay voice. 'Corporal Wallace is getting it now. Serve him bloody well right. We should have had his post. His dug-out'll be no good to him, though, if one of them jam-jars fall on it. Move to it. Build it up.'

'They'll die dry anyway,' grumbled a voice. 'Those — Lewis gunners always get whatever is going. Us bombers are treated like a lot of criminals. We mop up all the s—t. We're always stuck in front, a spy-escort, listening post. First in, last out.'

'Stop talking,' said the Corporal. 'Build it up.'

'Aye!' said another voice. 'Then when we get out, they tie us up, for fear we'd rob the canteen.'

Grumbling, they began to rebuild the parapet.

The sacks of earth, with which the parapet had been paved, had rotted. The earth in the sacks had been turned to slime by the rain. It was almost impossible to do anything with them. When a man lifted a sack it broke in two and the fragments fell, leaving foul slime on his hands. In the pitch darkness it was impossible for a man to see whether he was lifting a sack or a piece of rotten corpse. They cursed violently.

The sounds of their movements and of their voices,

uttering strange oaths, were uncouth in the darkness.

Eight Frenchmen had been killed by shell fire in that hole some time previously during an engagement. Their comrades, taking over the post under heavy fire, had used the shattered corpses as fortification.

'Better leave it to two men,' said a voice, after they worked without result for ten minutes.

'All right,' said the Corporal. 'Reilly, you and Gunn do the job. Get out of the way the rest of you. That bloody sniper we gave the cigarettes to yesterday had his eyes open all right. Can't trust one of those bastards.'

They all began to curse the sniper to whom they had given cigarettes the previous day and who had said: 'You no fire. All right. I no fire.' They cursed him, not because they believed that he had anything to do with the firing, but because somebody had to be blamed for the fall of the parapet, which caused work and a stink.

'It's all very well,' said a voice. 'It's no good — and blinding him now. When I wanted to shoot the — you blokes stopped me.'

'Don't start coming the old soldier, Reilly,' said the Corporal. 'Who's in charge of this post? You or me? I got orders not to allow any firing. You think you own this mob because you're a peace timer. Balls to you, drummer.'

'Good job if there were more peace wallahs knocking about,' said the voice. 'Bloody lot of rookies ...'

'What's your number, Reilly?' said the Corporal.

'Before you came up,' mumbled the voice.

'See you later,' said the Corporal. 'Who's that bloody-well groaning now? Somebody s—t himself?'

'It's Lamont, Corporal,' said a voice.

27

Lamont had again dug his face into the parapet.

Gunn dropped a sack and went over to him.

'He'll be all right, Corporal,' he said. 'Come on, kid.'

'What d'ye think you're on?' bawled the Corporal. 'A wet nurse? Get on with your work. Sweet Jesus! Why did You put this baby in my section? I didn't crucify You.'

'Oh! God Almighty!' moaned a voice. 'It's a wonder the ground doesn't open up and swallow us for that blasphemy.'

'Hear old preacher Appleby,' laughed a voice. 'The Holy Roller. Bloody old hypocrite.'

The Corporal went over to Lamont and pulled him away from the parapet.

'What's the matter with you?' he said.

Gunn, standing nearby, began to tremble and doubled his fists. At that moment he hated Lamont for his cowardice and yet intended to assault the Corporal in order to defend his mate. At the same time, a voice kept suggesting to him, very anxiously, that he should save himself from some awful catastrophe before it was too late.

Then Lamont raised his head and said in a querulous voice that amazed Gunn by its cool cunning:

'I've an awful pain in my stomach, Corporal.'

'I'll give you a pain somewhere else,' said the Corporal. 'Wait 'til we get out of the line. The M.O.'ll fix your guts all right. Stop moaning or I'll stuff my entrenching tool handle down your throat.'

Gunn breathed a sigh of relief and went back to his work.

'Christ!' said the Corporal. 'What a crew I've got!'

'That's the ticket,' said a voice. 'Blame us for the whole

bloomin' war while you're at it.'

The Corporal, aware that he was unable to keep order in the darkness, among this group of tough and discontented men, got very excited. He moved about, gave ridiculous orders and got everybody into a dreadful muddle. The military machine is kept working by the Corporal, the purpose of whose existence is to irritate the cogs under his control, keeping them continually active, irrespective of whether there is any purpose in their activity or not. So it was ordained by the designers of armies. But the designers had not foreseen, at least at that time, that groups of cogs, almost entirely cut off from the body of the machine, might lie in holes for days at a time, unable to find room for the senseless chores of which army routine is composed. Instead of producing that thoughtless bodily movement in response to orders, which characterises the good soldier, the Corporal now caused the exact opposite; simply because there was not enough room.

So that the nine men who babbled and staggered about in that sodden, water-logged, stinking hole, looked like nine lunatics, who, guided vaguely by a remnant of their former sanity, tried to keep in touch with the reality they had lost by an affectation of furious energy. They got in one another's way, knocked things out of one another's hands, cursed one another, asked questions, gave orders, picked things up and then dropped them again, sat down, got up again at once, scratched themselves, spat, shuddered and chattered continuously.

Suddenly a body was heard crawling up to the post from the rear. The Corporal cried out: 'Who's that?'

'That Corporal Williams?'

The Corporal instinctively brought his fists rigidly to his sides, as he answered:

'Sir-r-r-r!'

There was silence immediately. The droning of the rain became loud, as Lieutenant Bull, a huge figure in the gloom, panting loudly, like a primeval beast rising from the slime, slithered into the hole, bringing a little heap of mud after him with a clatter.

'Everybody all right here, Corporal?'

The officer's voice was bored and indifferent and his whole person exuded a feeling of boredom and indifference, in marked contrast to the nervousness of the men's voices and the furtive movements of their bodies. His breath smelt of whiskey. He carried a little, short stick, to help himself along through the mud.

Gunn gaped in the direction of the officer, just barely seeing him in the darkness. He felt terrified of him and was worried by this terror. Bull was the only officer in the company whom Gunn really liked. He felt towards him as towards a fellow human being. Bull was fearless. He was just. He did not treat his men as if they were children or pawns in a game of chess. He treated them as if they were really men and not cogs in a machine. He was ruthless and brutal in action; but behind the line he looked after his men with zeal, and protected their well-being with the same enthusiasm that a man would show towards expensive and cherished horses or hunting dogs.

He was the type of officer that a good soldier likes and respects. He had no pity for the inefficient or the cowardly. There was no sentiment in his nature. He was like a piston rod in a machine.

Until this moment, Gunn had always felt comforted by this officer's appearance in a trench. Now he felt afraid of him; sensing in himself the growth of something that the ruthless Lieutenant Bull would smash with his stick without a thought, or with a bullet from the heavy revolver he carried on his hip.

Gunn sought Lamont in the darkness with terrified eyes.

'Yes, sir,' said the Corporal. 'Everybody's all right here.'

'Parapet blown down, I see,' said the officer, stepping along the trench past the men, whom he brushed aside with his heavy body, without paying any more heed to them than if they were pieces of rubbish or indeed precious dogs.

They leaned back out of his way in awed silence, thrilled by the nearness of his body, which was covered by a uniform different from theirs.

His voice sounded horridly melancholy and remote, like the voice of a mumbling priest, who stands bored upon an altar before his fetish, while the devotees lie prostrate, worshipping both him and the fetish he so casually addresses in droning tones.

'Yes, sir,' said the Corporal. 'I'm getting it rebuilt.'

The Corporal's voice throbbed, addressing the officer.

The officer walked back again, saying:

'Get your men ready. We're going to advance. The enemy is retiring. Report to Company Headquarters for instructions in ... eh ...'

'Yes, sir.'

31

'Eh ... half an hour.'

'Yes, sir.'

The officer's bored and melancholy voice died away. He cleared his throat and slithered out of the hole. Casually, he stood up, rapped his thigh with his stick, stood still with bowed head for a few moments, as if thinking of something millions of miles away. Then he wandered away into the darkness. The men remained silent for a few moments and the rain made a loud sound, pattering on their steel hats and on the oil-sheets which they wore as cloaks.

Each man was saying to himself, 'We're going over the top. Will I come back?'

They had all been over the top except Lamont. They were all tough, hardened fighters; because of that, they knew and respected the dangers of an advance.

The Corporal, it being his business, called out to them cheerfully:

'Hear that, everybody? We're going over. He's retiring. We've got him on the run. That railhead rumour that the post corporal brought up must have been right. Jerry is chucking in his mitt. War over? Blimme!'

Everybody, except Lamont, got wildly excited, especially Gunn. Now that there was a prospect of action, something to do with his muscles and sinews, Gunn would not have to use his brain in combating the seductive temptation of his comrade. He became most excited in his ejaculations.

'Come on, boys,' he said. 'Let's have a last pot at them. Let's run 'em off the face of the earth. Up, the bloody bombing section!'

'He's retiring!' they cried, one after the other. 'He's beat. Blighty in a month!'

Shut in on a narrow sector of front, in fact, living in a lonely hole in No Man's Land, where a dark sky, sodden, naked earth and a curtain of droning rain constituted their world, they were incapable of comprehending the vastness of the army in which they formed the smallest unit. They were quite eager to believe, on the slightest encouragement, that the enemy had been defeated somewhere in a great battle and was now retiring, practically annihilated.

'All we have to do,' said one, 'is to run after him, mopping up his dug-outs.'

'Leave that parapet alone now,' said the Corporal. 'We won't need it. Next stop, Kaiser's palace in Berlin. Get ready those bombs and rifle grenades. Jump to it! Roll up your oil-sheets.'

They became as gay as schoolboys going on holiday; all except Lamont, who stood apart, silent. His large, blue eyes had become cunning, and his face had the strange cunning expression of a woman who is plotting something in secret.

Gunn went over to him and said:

'Well, matey! You'll get your baptism of fire tonight. Stick to me. I'll see you right. Then ... what price London?'

Lamont answered in a calm tone: 'Do you really believe the war is going to end?'

'Eh?' said Gunn, wrinkling his face in amazement at Lamont's sudden calmness.

'I don't believe the war is nearly over,' said Lamont, in the same curiously calm voice.

Gunn swore at him and moved away.

'I'm glad we're getting out of here, anyway,' said a gloomy voice. 'Although you blokes won't be as merry this time tomorrow as you are now.'

Several voices said:

'Aw! Chuck it, Reilly.'

'What are you grousing about now, Reilly?' said the Corporal. 'By cripes! I'll have you crimed for trying to demoralise the section.'

The gloomy voice again rose out of the dark hole, grumbling: 'This whole business is a trap. He ain't retiring.'

'Chuck it! Cut it out!' they murmured.

'If you ask me,' cried the gloomy voice in a louder tone, 'I don't believe one of us'll come back alive. Whenever I got into a post where men were buried it was unlucky.'

'Come on,' cried the Corporal, angrily. 'Get your rifle clean, Reilly, and close your trap. I'll take your number if you're not careful. What d'ye think you're on?'

Gunn went over and sat down beside Lamont. A stupid fellow, he was very superstitious and prone to be driven to the deepest despair or the wildest enthusiasm by the most trifling omen. Reilly, the gloomy old soldier, a man whom Gunn respected because he had been at the front since 1914, had said that a disaster was imminent. Then it must be imminent. He was almost as certain of it as if he had read it in a newspaper. At once, he connected Reilly's warning with Lamont's tempting.

Now, however, he felt tender towards Lamont. There must have been, he thought, a legitimate excuse for the boy's cowardly panic, when an old soldier like Reilly 'had the wind up'.

'Don't be afraid, lad,' he said, putting his hand on Lamont's shoulder. 'Pay no attention to old Reilly. It's only his old soldier's way of talking. There's no danger. Jerry is on the run.'

'I'm not paying any attention to him,' said Lamont, in his girlish voice. 'I know myself what is going to happen. My mind is made up. I feel happy now.'

'You do?' said Gunn in amazement. 'What about?'

'Shaw,' said the Corporal, 'you take charge here, while I'm away.'

'Yes, Corporal,' said a dignified voice.

'What d'you feel happy about?' repeated Gunn.

Lamont's voice broke as he said, 'Bill, I want you to write to mother for me when you come out of the line and tell her ...'

'Shut up,' muttered Gunn.

'Tell her that I ...'

'Shut up. Chuck it. Where's your rifle?'

He took Lamont's rifle and pretended to clean it.

'Listen,' he said. 'If we come hand-to-hand, don't forget ... see ... use the butt. Just raise the butt like that, upper cut. Then bash him on the head when he falls. Kill any man with a boot in the snout. Forget the bayonet. Eh?'

Lamont sighed. Gunn suddenly bit his lower lip until it bled, threw Lamont's rifle on the fire-step and moved away to empty his bladder in the corner.

The Corporal came back. He was nervous.

'Looks a big job,' he said. 'The whole brigade is going over.'

Although they could not see his face, they felt the nervousness in his voice. They also became nervous.

Now the battle front had again become silent. The melancholy droning of the rain and the flopping of mud clods into shell holes were the only sounds.

Suddenly Gunn's voice rose loudly from the hole, crying, 'By God! I'm going to make some bastard suffer for this rain. I'll spill some bastard's blood before long.'

Silence followed this outburst.

'What's the matter with him?' whispered a voice.

'Hey! Hey!' said the Corporal. 'You going off your chump?'

'Nothing the matter with me,' said Gunn, in a queer tone.

In spite of his words, he felt that there was something queer the matter with him. He felt a pain in his eye sockets, and he kept shutting his eyes in order to hide from little balls of fire that kept approaching him from out the darkness.

'Damn-all the matter with me,' he repeated with stupid arrogance.

Chapter Three

Just before dawn, Corporal Williams led his men out of the post into No Man's Land. All told, they numbered nine souls.

No. 7946 Corporal John Williams, leading, was a sallow-faced man, with a long, thin neck and a wide, low forehead. He was six feet one inch in height. His limbs were loose and nervous in their movements. His hands were flabby and hot to the touch. His eyes were pale and watery. They varied in expression, at one time furtive and terror-stricken, at another cunning and determined. He moved like an eel. He was servile to his superiors, arrogant and cruel to his subordinates. Although he was extremely diligent in his duties and a severe disciplinarian, his company commander disapproved of him. His failure to attain promotion had made him very bitter. In civilian life he had been a grocer's assistant. He was twenty-nine years old. He had served two years and twenty-four days.

No. 8740 Private George Appleby followed the Corporal. He had been a labourer in a chocolate factory as a civilian. He was a fanatical believer in the doctrines of an obscure Christian sect, whose members encourage hysteria in their religious observances. His former work and his creed injured his constitution and made it impossible for him to become a really efficient soldier, although he was powerfully built, with a dogged courage that made him worthy of serving in the ranks of that famous regiment. He was too fat about the face and body. His complexion was yellowish. His cheeks were puffy. He moved stiffly, like an old dray-horse. All his organs were functioning inefficiently. He was of a morbid disposition and never laughed. He always muttered prayers, even on parade. He was thirty years old. He was commonly called 'The Preacher', or 'The Holy Roller'. He had served two years and ten days.

No. 9087 Private Michael Friel followed Appleby. He was a lean, slim man, with red hair, a freckled face and blue eyes. He had been a policeman in civilian life. He stammered slightly when excited and he constantly wore an expression of great worry, as if his mind were engaged in unravelling very intricate problems. Although an excellent soldier behind the line, he was unreliable in action, as he had utterly no initiative and really had a streak of cowardice in him. He was a very silent fellow. He never mixed with his section comrades behind the line, always consorting with a man in No. 4 Platoon who had also been a policeman. He corresponded with three women and was very proud of his person. He had once been a sergeant but had been reduced to the ranks for breaking camp one night and lying with a French whore until after reveille. He had served one year and 287 days.

He was twenty-seven years old. His height was five feet eleven inches.

No. 11145 Private Simon Jennings followed Friel. This soldier was serving under an assumed name. He had formerly been an officer in the Army Service Corps but had been cashiered for forging a cheque. He was the younger son of a bishop and had led a very dissipated life, principally on the score of drunkenness, gambling and lechery. Although he was a poor soldier and unable to keep his uniform or equipment in proper condition, his intelligence was often of assistance in moments of stress. His manner and personal habits endeared him to his comrades, who respected him because he had once been an officer; but more especially because he received an allowance, about which he was very generous. His mottled face and bleary eyes bore witness to the life he had led. He was getting bald and he had legs like an old man. When under the influence of drink, he preached a new form of christianity, which was mainly based on pacifism and 'Universal, scientific, ethical co-operation', as he quaintly described it. The officers all disliked him. He had served in this regiment for one year 110 days. He was five feet ten inches in height. He was nicknamed 'The Gent'.

No. 8637 Private Jeremiah McDonald followed Jennings. He had been a farm labourer in civilian life. He was a bony, uncouth fellow, with an ape-like face, outstanding ears, a short thick nose and stupid grey eyes. His knuckles were very large. There was hardly any flesh on his bones. He was the butt of the company owing to his stupidity, his gluttony and his incapacity for performing correctly even the simplest movements of military drill. Because he was always picked for sanitary fatigue, they nicknamed him 'Crap'. He had served for two years and twenty-seven days. He was exactly six feet in height and thirty-four years old.

No. 4048 Private Daniel Reilly followed McDonald. This man was an excellent soldier, but owing to his taste for drink and his peculiar temperament, he had never risen from the ranks. He had never done any useful labour in civilian life, having served as a tout for a street bookmaker at one time, and at another time as chucker-out in an illicit drinking shop which was also a brothel. He had been seven years and sixty-four days in the service. He was a dark fellow, with very shrewd, dark eyes and a countenance that seemed to express innocence, simplicity and candour. He wore drooping, black moustaches. He was never without money, as he had a regular organisation for the collection and disposal of loot. He respected nothing in search for loot and was known to have dug up and robbed an airman, who crashed head first into the muddy ground, sinking to the heels of his boots. He was five feet ten inches in height. He had been at the front since the outbreak of war, but had never been wounded. He found great pleasure in foretelling disaster.

No. 8365 Private William Gunn followed Reilly. He was officially described at headquarters as a general labourer, thirty-three years of age, six feet two inches in height, marked by a crushed right ear and a scar on the left cheekbone, with service of two years and thirty-four days.

No. 12468 Private Louis Lamont followed Gunn. He was officially described as a student, nineteen years of age, five feet nine inches in height, with service of 310 days.

No. 3920 Private James Shaw brought up the rear. He had served for nine years and eighty-one days, and was the most reliable and cunning soldier, not only in the section, but in the battalion. His whole body was covered with wounds. He had three bayonet scars on his face. His head was completely bald. He was stoutly built and was immensely strong. His face and neck were exactly the colour of an old penny. He had risen twice to the rank of sergeant but had lost his stripes each time through drink. He was prone to fits of melancholy and could never sleep more than two hours at a stretch. He often spent whole nights sitting on his blankets, smoking his pipe and thinking. He was a champion billiard player. He had very long, black eyelashes and a beautiful tenor voice. He was the most respected soldier in the company. The company officer always chose him for dangerous work. He had been decorated for valour three times. He was five feet ten inches in height. His civilian occupation was officially described as that of an excise officer.

These nine men, under the command of Corporal John Williams, went over the top a little before dawn on the morning of March 20th, 1917.

Chapter Four

It still rained. As soon as they stepped out into No Man's Land, they sank into the mud to their ankles. They advanced in file, their rifles at the high port, their bayonets fixed, their gas masks at the ready. They floundered about, groaning at each step, dragged down by the sticky mud, by the cumbersome weight of their rain-sodden greatcoats and by their war equipment, rifles, entrenching tools, bullets, bombs, rifle-grenades, rations, Verey lights, wire-cutters, gas masks. They rattled and clanked, like armoured ghosts, slopping and clucking and groaning through the mud.

The Corporal had received orders to advance in a straight line and occupy the section of the enemy's front line that faced the outpost. The distance was given to him as approximately 350 paces. It appeared to be simple enough before they left the post, because the parapet of the post faced the enemy. But as soon as they left the post and had advanced about twenty yards the Corporal sidestepped to avoid a clump of barbed wire. He went on another five yards and then halted, realising that he did not know where he was.

Appleby, following immediately behind, gloomily indifferent to where he was going and praying under his breath, stumbled against the Corporal. They both fell into the mud. Friel came up and, before he could halt, fell over Appleby. As he fell, he lowered the point of his bayonet, instinctively trying to save himself. He fleshed the Corporal slightly on the buttocks.

'Halt!' whispered Jennings.

They all halted, one after the other. Being trained soldiers, as soon as they moved out of their hole, they ceased to think of anything except the business in hand, which consisted solely in placing one foot carefully in front of the other and in keeping their eyes fixed on the centre of the back of the man in front. The Corporal, being in command, was thinking for them. They were half-asleep. Now, finding that something had gone wrong and that they had to halt, a fact for which no provision had been made, they awakened in a startled fashion. In their excitement, they broke ranks and got into a bunch.

The Corporal, lying on the ground with Appleby across his back, began to mutter curses, spluttering and spitting forth the mud which got into his mouth. He reached out and struck Appleby a smart blow with the butt of his rifle. He thought it was Appleby who had prodded him with the bayonet.

Appleby squealed, 'I'm wounded.'

'I'll wound you, you bastard,' growled the Corporal, giving him another whack. 'What's your number?'

'What's on now?' grumbled Shaw from the rear. 'Move on. We don't want to get caught here.'

Lamont leaned on Gunn and whispered, 'I'm dead beat. I can go no farther.'

The Corporal and Appleby were still on the ground arguing. Appleby was swearing that it was not he who had stuck the Corporal. The Corporal swore that it was. Friel, like the cute fellow he was, had at once struggled to his feet as soon as he had done the damage and got out of the way. He fell in behind Jennings.

'What's the idea, Friel?' said Jennings. 'Where are you going?'

'Don't stick your blasted rifle in my face, you,' cried Gunn, digging his elbow into McDonald's face.

'Cripes!' said McDonald, staggering against Friel.

The Corporal got to his feet and cried in a loud whisper, 'Move on. Stop that whispering.'

Everybody took a step and then stopped. They were going in six different directions.

'We're lost,' said Reilly. 'What did I say? I told you so.'

'Keep together,' said the Corporal. 'Don't wander about. Come on.'

They moved on.

Suddenly there was a heavy splash. Jennings fell head first into a shell hole, having tripped over a barbed-wire stake. Friel tripped over the stake also but saved himself. As he called out, 'Mind the stake,' he was pushed from behind by McDonald right into the shell hole on top of Jennings.

'Help!' cried Jennings. 'I'm drowned.'

'What's up now?' said the Corporal. 'Halt!'

'Pull them out,' said Reilly. 'They're sure to drown. Come on, lads, don't stand looking at them. There were four Jocks drowned like that relieving the Froggies at Sailly.'

'Who's in that shell hole?' said the Corporal, staggering over. 'Get out of that hole.'

'I can't bloody well get out,' muttered McDonald. 'Let go of my scabbard, Gent.'

'Where the hell are you?' said Gunn, stooping over the hole. 'Catch the end of my rifle.'

'God!' said Jennings. 'I've lost my rifle.'

'Fish it out, then,' said the Corporal. 'You're not much good with a rifle, but you're worse without one.'

They spent over ten minutes dragging McDonald and Jennings out of the hole. Jennings came out without his rifle.

'Go in again and get it,' said the Corporal.

Jennings, shivering and shaking himself like a wet hen, was covered from head to foot in slime.

'I'd die, Corporal,' he said. 'I'm all in.'

Gunn cursed and said he would go in for it.

'Get out of my way,' he said.

He stepped into the hole, searched around with his foot, got the rifle and hauled it out. He handed it to Jennings.

'Thank you,' said Jennings. 'But how am I ever going to get it clean?'

'Everybody all right now?' said the Corporal. 'Get in your proper places.'

They floundered about until they were in line.

'Who's that sitting down there?' said the Corporal. 'Fall in that man. Who told you to sit down? What is your number?'

'I was tying my puttee, Corporal,' said Lamont in his girlish voice.

'Oh! Christ!' said the Corporal. 'There he is again. The principal boy, tightening her tights. Get up, you little bastard.'

Lamont got up. He had not really been doing anything but had sat down for a rest. He fell in behind Gunn.

'Hang on to my scabbard,' whispered Gunn, 'and give me your rifle.'

'Say, Corporal,' said Appleby. 'I think we're going wrong.'

'Shut up, you fool,' said the Corporal. 'Eh? Where are we? All right! I've got it. Move on.'

Again they advanced, floundering, for about ten yards and then Shaw cried out, 'Hey! Where are we going? That's our post there. We're on the wrong side of it.'

'Halt!' said the Corporal.

He came over to Shaw. The latter pointed to the top of the elephant frame which covered the extreme left of the post.

'See that?' said he.

'Where? Where?' said the Corporal, peering.

Shaw tipped the zinc with the butt of his rifle. The Corporal swore.

'Turn back,' he said, moving up to the front of the line.

They all turned about, lost their positions and got into a bunch, arguing and cursing.

'Get into your right places, ' said the Corporal. 'Get ... Oh! God!'

Although there were only nine of them all told it seemed impossible to form a line. The Corporal pushed them and threatened to take their numbers, but only added to the confusion by his exhortations and threats. Catching Lamont by his shoulders to put him into his place, he noticed the boy had no rifle.

'Where's your rifle?' he said.

'I've got his rifle, Corporal,' said Gunn.

'Give it to him, you daft bastard,' said the Corporal. 'Did you ever hear of a man going over the top with a servant to carry his rifle? Gunn, I'll report you for this.'

'What have I done?' said Gunn angrily. 'It was only ...'

'Don't answer me back,' said the Corporal. 'As for you, Lamont, your mother won't know you when I've done with you.'

'Chuck that, Corporal!' said Gunn with great violence. 'Leave the kid's mother out of it.'

The Corporal thrust his face near to Gunn's face and said, 'Eh? Say that again. D'ye know what you're saying?'

In the darkness, the face of each appeared enormous to the other's eyes. They could not see one another's eyes. But they could hear one another's breathing and smell one another. Gunn stood very stiffly, with his heart thumping. The Corporal leant forward with his jaws strained upwards, grasping his rifle with both hands, threatening.

Although Gunn did not speak and although he stood rigid in a respectful attitude, the Corporal became afraid of the man and as a consequence began at that moment to hate him.

Gunn also began to hate the Corporal.

Without saying anything further the Corporal moved away to the head of the section, forgetting that Gunn still carried Lamont's rifle, which he had ordered Gunn to return to its owner. The men moved on.

There was silence for some time. Gunn kept grinding his teeth. He was struggling to overcome his hatred of the Corporal, or rather, the terrible inclination towards the commission of a certain act that was inspired by this hatred. Lamont, clinging to his empty bayonet scabbard for support, now appeared to him as something unpleasant which he really detested but was forced to protect for an occult reason.

'How utterly idiotic!' said Jennings suddenly. 'Nobody seems to know where we are going.'

'No talking now,' said the Corporal. 'We're getting near his line.'

'We are like hell,' said Reilly.

'Who's that?' said a voice from the right.

They all halted.

'No. 2 Bombers,' said the Corporal. 'Is that Corporal Wallace?'

'Yes,' said the voice. 'Where are we?'

'How the hell do I know?' said Corporal Williams. 'Wait there. I'm coming over. Come on, lads.'

The bombers floundered across to Corporal Wallace's Lewis gunners.

'I halted here,' said Corporal Wallace, 'and sent a man out to look for you, but he hasn't come back. Did you see him?'

'No. We're lost, I think. Whereabouts are you?'

'I don't know. I thought you might know. Are you far from your post?'

'Can't say. Are you far from your post?'

'I don't know where I am.'

They began to argue about their position and about the orders which they had received. The men of both sections, delighted at being able to talk to one another after a separation of two days, eagerly asked questions.

'What was it like in your post?'

'Bloody awful. Dusty Smith got back yesterday, sick. Any of your chaps hit in that firing?'

'Yes. '38 Finnigan got a packet in the back. Shrap.'

'Lucky bastard!'

They were indifferent to the business they had in hand and discussed their little affairs, like gossiping old men, while the Corporals, being in charge, shouldering all the responsibility for the extraordinary situation in which they and their men were placed, lost in No Man's Land, argued about the direction of the enemy's front line.

It was all to no purpose. In the pitch darkness, orders, officers, Sergeant-Majors, trenches, positions and the enemy, with his rival organisation of officers, orders, trenches and positions, all disappeared and became meaningless, just as reality becomes transformed in a wild nightmare. They were lost in No Man's Land, floundering in the mud, while the ceaseless rain fell upon them with a monotonous drone.

Mud, rain, darkness and babbling men!

Unable to think of any intelligent solution of their difficulty, the two Corporals decided to join forces. They marched off together in what they considered was a new direction. They soon entered a space which was covered with barbed wire entanglements. Appleby tripped over a stake, hurtled forward and fell prone on the wire. He immediately began to moan in his gloomy voice, 'I'm wounded. I'm wounded.'

'The curse of God on you, Appleby,' said Corporal Williams. 'What is the matter with you now? Have you fallen into another shell hole?'

The ground was wired in patches and the Corporal had got through the entanglement on an open space. But as he stepped back to see what was the matter with Appleby, he himself got caught and fell.

Now several voices cried out 'Mind the wire. Look out!'

Trying to evade the wire, they nearly all got caught on it, as they instinctively got together in a bunch for protection. Their voices rose almost to a shout, in spite of the Corporals, who shouted still louder than the men, ordering silence. There was an uproar, like a brawl in a tavern.

Appleby, on being dragged away from the wire, was found to be gashed severely along the right thigh. A man of the Lewis gun section had his face cut. The Corporal's right arm was slightly torn. The others escaped with torn clothes. They bandaged the injured and set forth once more, in search of the enemy's front line.

Now there was no attempt at falling in by sections or moving in file. Although the two Corporals, from sheer force of habit, still whispered commands and threats, nobody took any notice. They had lost all semblance of discipline, and indeed they had quite forgotten about the enemy and about the war.

Now they only feared the darkness and the mud and the falling rain; and they desired feverishly to reach the enemy's line as a refuge from the horrid wilderness in which they were lost.

Gunn got separated from Lamont during the confusion at the entanglements. He still carried the youth's rifle slung on his shoulder. In his brain he carried the knowledge that he hated the Corporal.

Now, as he floundered along through the mud, concealed from observation by the darkness, this hatred took complete possession of him, distorting his features, making his brain hot, stiffening his muscles, causing his chest to expand and contract painfully, making his blood tingle.

Suddenly another voice hailed them.

'Who's that?'

Both Corporals answered.

'Where the blasted hell are you?' came the voice.

It was Platoon Sergeant Corcoran. They halted and waited for him to come up. He had Corporal Tynan's section with him.

'How the hell did you get here?' he said, angrily.

Now the Sergeant and the three Corporals began to argue. Then they all set out together. A few minutes later they were joined by the fourth section of the platoon. Another argument followed. Then the whole platoon set out to seek the enemy's front line, cursing, groaning, falling into shell holes, getting caught on barbed wire, utterly exhausted.

Dawn came. Somebody cried out suddenly, 'See. There it is.'

They saw the enemy's front line within a few yards of them. They gaped at it like small boys who have for the first time reached a hill distant from their village, and found to their amazement that it's not an imposing mountain but a dull hillock. This long, winding hole had, a few hours before, contained dangerous enemies. It was a secure place, fortified with parapets, with comfortable dug-outs, a place that aroused envy in them, as they lay in shallow exposed holes. Now it was deserted, a morass, half-full of debris.

The enemy had destroyed everything. Where dug-outs had been sunk deep into the ground there were now quagmires. Planks, old iron, sheets of zinc, pieces of concrete littered the ground.

They stepped down into this trench, with their weapons pointed foolishly, although there was not even a rat to oppose them. They spread out at the Sergeant's command and then stood still. There was nothing to do.

Word was passed along after a delay of twenty minutes, 'We are to wait here for orders.'

It still rained.

Then a groan of anger passed along the line. Sodden with rain, torn by barbed wire, hungry, bloodshot in the eyes from want of sleep, lousy, they suddenly became enraged with this foolish expedition in the darkness from one hole to another; an expedition that now seemed utterly without purpose.

It was a groan of revolt against Authority, but it had no power behind it. It was rather like the revolt of an over-laden ass, which, when whipped under his load by a cruel and stupid master, tosses his foolish ears and grinds his teeth; but afterwards, groaning, with downcast head, goes on until he falls.

Chapter Five

It was at that moment that Gunn first allowed his hatred for the Corporal to assert itself in action.

He was standing stiffly erect, in his torn, muddy great-coat, laden with accoutrements, motionless, with his bayoneted rifle in his hands, looking out across the parados of the enemy trench, towards a long low hill, beyond which the enemy had retired. Night had now changed into day; but there was hardly any light and the naked earth looked still more melancholy than when it was concealed by the darkness. Its ugliness was exposed.

When he heard the groaning of his comrades his reason suddenly overbalanced. It was like the blow of a whip urging him to revolt. As he listened to its sound, he had a strange vision. At first he shuddered. Then he felt a sharp pain in his ears. He closed his eyes and saw a dark cave in which a man was prowling about with a club. Afar off, somewhere in the cave, seals were moaning and flopping about on rocks and tumbling into unseen pools, while, from the roof of the cave, brine water fell with a droning sound on slippery rocks.

He opened his eyes and shrugged himself. He heard the moaning of his comrades and the droning of the rain, as it fell on his steel helmet and on a sheet of zinc which lay in a puddle before him to the rear of the trench. He heard the flopping sound of feet moving about in water.

Then he closed his eyes again and saw the man clubbing the seals as they came towards him; smashing their blubbery skulls.

He started and opened his eyes. Impelled by a savage and irresistible impulse, he leaned forward, rested his rifle against the sheet of zinc and fired several times at the hill in front.

Then his brain cleared. He felt afraid and said to himself, 'My God! What's the matter with me? What am I doing?'

At once he thought of the Corporal.

Everybody looked at Gunn and several men instinctively pointed their rifles at the hill, thinking there were enemies in sight. Sergeant Corcoran came running along from the right.

'Who fired that shot?' he cried, angrily.

Gunn stood still, looking to his front. He did not reply. The shock of discovering that he was beginning to lose control of himself had passed. Now he felt a cunning delight in something vague and mysterious; some intention that was yet unnamed. He was laughing within himself. He did not reply. With his flattened ear, his scarred cheek, his thick neck, his heavy lips, his body that was like a full sack, standing as straight as a pillar, he looked like a statue of Stupidity. There was no sign of thought on his bronzed face, nor in his unblinking eyes.

He appeared to be exactly the same as he had been a few hours before, standing in the outpost, advising Lamont against the shame of cowardice and disloyalty to his soldier's oath. But he had entirely changed inside him. He had become subtle. Evil!

'Who fired those shots?' cried Corporal Williams, rushing along the trench from the left.

Gunn smiled slightly without replying. But he said to himself:

'That's him. Let him come.'

Others cried out on either side:

'Who fired those shots?'

Then, again, Gunn became afraid, as the two non-commissioned officers approached. Again his ears pained him. He lost his subtlety. His brain clouded. His thoughts became confused. His eyes opened wider. His lips moved nervously. His heart throbbed violently. He felt a thickness in his throat and he saw that some disaster was impending. Then he could not restrain himself from crying out in a loud voice: 'I fired the bloody shots. What the hell do you blokes think you are here for? Eh?'

'It's you again, Gunn,' bawled the Corporal, coming up with his fist doubled. 'I'll give you firing, you cock-eyed, clumsy rookie. Is that what you're up to, trying to draw fire on us ? Haven't you got any intelligence? Didn't you hear the order?'

Gunn stared at the Corporal, breathing heavily, swaying back and forth. His eyes became blurred and he had a curious hallucination that the Corporal was becoming transformed into a hairy animal; a brute which he wanted to kill.

That terrified him. He became craven, as he remembered the dreadful consequences of such an act. He rubbed his eyes with the sleeve of his greatcoat, saw the Corporal in his exact proportions and began to blubber something inaudible.

'Silence!' yelled the Corporal. 'Don't answer me back.'

'Who fired those shots?' said Sergeant Corcoran, coming up.

'It's Gunn, Sergeant,' said the Corporal. 'Here he is. Look at him.'

'Take his number,' said the Sergeant. 'Put him in the book. Hey, you! What's the idea? By Jesus! I'll put wheels under you.'

All Gunn's fury withered away, like the ashes of a burnt fire blown by the wind. He felt limp, empty, weak, before these two men, who stood with their faces close to his, threatening him with their fists, shouting foul abuse at him. It was not they who annihilated him but the authority they represented, the great machine that stretched, covering the whole battle front, like a sprawling colossus. Authority!

In his simplicity, he was at that moment certain that 'It' could read his mind and discover the germs of revolt that had come to life in his mind.

The two N.C.O.s were not so much excited by the offence he had committed as by a desire to terrify the others through bullying Gunn. They knew that the muttering of the men could best be silenced by making an example of Gunn. They wanted to use Gunn as a butt for maintaining the iron discipline which is necessary to make soldiers suffer the unspeakable tortures and indignities of war with resignation. They tapped him with their knuckles and with their rifle butts. They kicked his shins, as if he were a horse, at which one shouts 'lift' when his hoofs are wrongly placed. They pulled his uniform about. They pulled at his rifle. They examined his ammunition pouches, his gas mask, his haversack. They accused him of having eaten his iron rations, of being deficient of his field dressing, of having fouled his uniform, of having an obscene disease.

The Sergeant, being an old soldier and a drill sergeant during peace-time, was superior to the Corporal at this astounding business of persecution. He was a lean, dandified fellow, with a Kaiser moustache and bright blue eyes like a woman. His voice was as shrill and sharp as that of a starling. Every second word he uttered was an oath or obscene.

'Look at him!' he cried. 'Call himself a soldier? A farmer wouldn't hire him to frighten crows out of a cornfield. Take him for disorderly dress, Corporal. Don't answer me back. Take him for answering back, Corporal.'

Gunn had not uttered a word.

'Stand to attention!' cried the Sergeant. 'Take him for insolence.'

Gunn had been standing to attention but had been thrown off his balance when the Sergeant punched him violently in the chest.

Then Appleby hailed the Sergeant from the right, saving Gunn from further persecution.

'Sergeant!' he called, 'Corporal Wallace wants to speak to you.'

'All right,' said the Sergeant, moving away from Gunn, without any emotion, as casually as if he had just stopped to say good morning to the man. 'Corporal Williams, get your men to clean their rifles and mop up this trench. Jump to it.'

'Yes, Ser'nt.'

The Sergeant stepped briskly on his thin, elegant legs around the corner of a traverse to the right. He called back, 'Corporal Williams, you had better keep order in your section. If those shots draw fire on this position, you'll be for it. The whole platoon is not going to suffer for ... All right! All right! I'm coming. What the bleedin' hell is the matter here?'

Corporal Williams put his notebook in his pocket and said to Gunn, 'By Jesus! Wait till I get you out of the line. You'll be for it. I'll make you hop. It's No. 1 for the duration.'

He pushed his clenched fist close to Gunn's face and called him by an obscene name. Gunn made no reply or movement of resistance to this final insult. He was no longer a man, six feet two inches in height, with a thick neck, powerful jaws and a body like a full sack, the strongest man in that company of strong men, a fearless soldier in battle. He was now like the dead carcass of an animal, propped up.

Now the Corporal did not fear Gunn as he had feared him during the night when they stood face to face in No Man's Land. He saw no hatred and no revolt in Gunn's eyes. He saw only the brutal submission of the flogged slave.

He turned away, arrogantly, his mean soul exalted by the fact that he had successfully baited and bullied into submission a man stronger and braver than himself.

Chapter Five

'Come on, lads,' he said. 'Jump to it. Clean your rifles and ammunition. Mop up this trench.'

'Which are we to do first?' said Reilly.

'Mop up the trench,' said the Corporal. 'Be careful of anything suspicious-looking you see lying around.'

Mechanically and subdued, the men moved about, mopping up the trench. They had no shred of intelligence left owing to their exhaustion. They just wandered about helplessly, picking things up in one place and putting them down in another place, where they were picked up again and put down once more.

'Mop it up,' the Corporal kept saying.

He himself was almost as exhausted and stupid as the others and just wandered, bobbing his head back and forth on his thin neck like a goose.

The men spread out, peering into destroyed dug-outs, into bays and down communication trenches. It was dangerous to go too far, as half the place was a quagmire into which a man could sink twenty feet. Nobody spoke. They were almost asleep, staggering, with their eyes nearly closed.

Gunn, wandering about, came upon Lamont. As soon as he had landed in the trench, Lamont had got into a corner and sat down to rest. He had the instinct of a born malingerer, always avoiding work and concealing himself from the observation of his superiors. Now there was no trace of panic in his beautiful blue eyes. He seemed perfectly at his ease. He was gnawing a piece of biscuit.

Gunn looked at him. He felt terribly ashamed now, in the presence of the youth, at the memory of the humiliation he had just suffered.

'Did you hear that?' he said.

'What?' said Lamont, looking up with indifference.

'Didn't you hear the bawling off I got?' said Gunn.

'Yes! I heard something,' said the youth, casually. 'Was it you they were talking to? Why did you fire? You shouldn't have fired.'

'Eh?' said Gunn, in amazement.

His eyes grew large and he opened his mouth. He wiped his face on his sleeve.

'That little bastard!' he said. 'He doesn't give a damn if they put me up against the parapet and shoot me.'

'You're a cool one,' he said, aloud. 'Blowed, but you are. I get myself bawled off over you and then you ... Blast it! It all happened over you last night. See? I'm finished with you from now on. I'll have no more to do with you. What are you skiving there for? Can't you muck in and mop up the trench?'

Now Gunn hated the youth and was amazed at himself for having been such a fool as to defend him, work for him and suffer the mockery of the platoon on his account, for the past three months. This little fellow with the damned subtlety and insincerity of a woman!

'By God!' he said, 'never again will I be taken in by you. There's nothing the matter with you now. Last night you were on the point of ...'

'What's on here?' cried the Corporal, sticking his head around a corner. 'What are you doing here, Gunn. Did I tell you to mop up this trench?'

Gunn moved off. Lamont got to his feet. He dropped his quizzical, sly expression in a flash. His face became pathetic; as humbly melancholy as that of a little barefooted street Arab, begging a penny from a woman.

'Get out of my bloomin' sight,' said the Corporal, 'before I murder you.'

Lamont shuddered and moved after Gunn.

'Say, Bill,' he said, 'you're not cross, are you?'

Gunn turned on him angrily, saw his pathetic face and felt sorry for having been rough with him.

'Say, Bill,' said Lamont, 'would you like a bit of that cake I got from mother. Half of it is yours, you know. She told me to share it equally with you. There's some left yet.'

'I don't want your bloody cake,' said Gunn, moving away again.

Lamont followed him.

'Where did you get your rifle?' said Gunn. 'Eh? I didn't give it back to you. How did you get it?'

'Yes. You gave it back to me when we got here,' said Lamont. 'Don't you remember?'

'I don't remember,' said Gunn. 'That's queer.'

He stared at Lamont.

'My God!' he said to himself. 'There must be something the matter with me.'

'What the hell are you following me about for?' he said, aloud.

The youth stared at him in silence. His lower lip began to tremble.

Gunn swore and then, conquered by his inability to rid himself of this incubus, Lamont, he said: 'All right then. Hang on to me. Help me, Christ! I'll look after you.'

Suddenly a voice shrieked.

'Ha!' said Gunn. 'That's Appleby.'

Reilly, who was nearby, shaking a wickered cask that

he found, looked up and said, 'There's some left in this yoke. Wonder have they poisoned it? It's beer, I think.'

'Isn't that Appleby that shouted?' said Gunn.

'Wonder would it be dangerous to touch it?' said Reilly.

'Help! Help!' cried Appleby in the distance.

There was an extraordinary note of terror in his voice.

'Oh, Christ! What has he done now?' said Friel.

The Corporal ran past. Reilly, still shaking the cask, suggested an obscene reason for Appleby's cry. They all laughed, except Gunn, who stood with his head on his chest and his underlip protruding, saying to himself:

'I must pull myself together. I mustn't let it get hold of me.'

As soon as he had again come under the influence of his affection for Lamont, his hatred of the Corporal returned.

'Where are you, Appleby?' shouted the Corporal on the right.

Gunn started and said aloud, 'There he is.'

'Eh?' said Friel, stopping, as he passed Gunn, on his way to Appleby's assistance. 'Who?'

Gunn looked at Friel and said fiercely, 'I didn't say anything.'

Friel looked at Gunn curiously and thought, 'He's getting queer.'

Then he passed on. Gunn thoughtlessly followed him. Now he did not know what he was doing. There was a sharp pain at the rear of his skull.

When the Corporal reached the spot where Appleby had been posted to mop up, there was no sign of the man. Neither was he crying out any longer. A few minutes previously the Corporal had left him in an island traverse, to the rear of which there was a quagmire, caused by the demolition of a large dug-out. Then the Corporal rounded the corner of the traverse, stepping over a heap of planks, empty casks, broken boxes, torn sacks and wire netting. He uttered a cry of horror. In a circular quagmire, about ten feet in diameter, he saw Appleby, sinking slowly.

The unfortunate man had already sunk to his thighs. In his right hand he held his rifle and bayonet. When he fell, he had reached out with his weapon, striving to stick the bayonet into a pile of sandbags that lay on the far brink of the hole. The bayonet had not reached the sacks and had landed on the quagmire. There also, near the sacks, lay what the wretched man had plunged into the quagmire to attain — two tins of canned meat. Goaded by hunger, he had momentarily forgotten the death trap that lay between him and his trivial booty. Instead of dropping his rifle when the bayonet point had missed the bank, he held on to it by a soldierly instinct, thereby weighing down his body; while, at the same time, he reached out with his left hand, backwards, towards the opposite bank of the quagmire. Now he was clawing the air with his left hand. His face had gone yellow. His chest was heaving in a queer fashion; remaining expanded for a long time and then contracting with great speed. His eyes bulged. His lips moved in prayer. Intermittently his back curved and writhed like that of a badly wounded animal. Hoarse sounds issued from his throat. The fingers of his left hand opened and closed slowly like the seemingly unguided movements of a worm tossing its head, or a snail moving its horns.

The Corporal stood for a few moments looking at him open-mouthed, so horrified by the sight that he could not comprehend the situation.

'What the bloody hell are you doing there?' he said. 'Get out of that.'

Appleby twisted his head towards the Corporal, saw him and then moved his lips to speak. Instead of speaking he stuck out his tongue at the Corporal. His tongue lolled on his lower lip. His mouth fell wide open. The tongue became still. He was speechless and almost paralysed with fear. He was now buried to the waist, suddenly drawn down more quickly by the movement he had made to face the Corporal.

Realising that the man was really drowning, the Corporal thrust forward his rifle, crying, 'Catch that.' At the same time he called out, 'Help! Man drowning.'

The muzzle of the Corporal's rifle was within reach of Appleby's left hand. Instead of catching it with that hand, however, he dropped his own rifle and twisted his body round so as to be able to grip the Corporal's rifle with both hands. The result was that he caught the gun with violence, using the last of his strength for the effort. He pulled it towards him and dragged the Corporal into the hole. As he fell, the Corporal dropped the rifle, uttered a cry, turned about, gasped and threw himself forward on his chest. He thrust out his right hand and gripped the end of a plank that protruded from the wall of the trench.

Appleby, now making a gurgling sound in his throat, sank to his armpits.

Just then Friel, followed by Gunn, reached the brink of the quagmire.

'A hand! A hand!' cried the Corporal, seeing them.

'God Almighty!' said Friel, standing stock still.

Gunn, without a moment's hesitation, pushed Friel aside and gripped the Corporal's hand.

'Help! Help!' cried Friel, standing foolishly on the bank, staring at Appleby.

Gunn hauled at the Corporal's hand so violently that he nearly wrenched the arm from its socket. The Corporal groaned with pain. His body, lying doubled up in the quagmire, with his thighs near his chest, was sinking by the stern and had already become embedded. Gunn, in spite of having pulled with all his strength, had not moved the body an inch.

Reilly had now come up and, immediately realising the situation, called out to Gunn: 'Just hold him. Don't pull.'

'God!' said Friel, who still stood idly on the bank, gaping at Appleby, as if hypnotised. 'Look at Appleby. Hey! Appleby! Appleby!'

Reilly yelled into Friel's ear, 'Get your bloody equipment off. Hey! Lads! Shaw! Come on. Hold him Gunn. Corporal Wallace! Ho, there! Keep your head up, Corporal. Friel ... your bloody ... off with ... I say ... equipment ... equipment.'

'Give me your hand, Corporal,' said Gunn.

'No, don't stir,' said Reilly. 'Lie still, Corporal.'

'Jesus! He's gone,' said Friel. 'Look at Appleby.'

'Don't mind him,' said Reilly. 'Get off your equipment.'

No. 8740 Private George Appleby, formerly a worker in a chocolate factory, recently a member of the bombing section of No. 2 Platoon, at that moment ceased to exist as a living organism. He had thrown back his head and stared at the sky with fixed eyes, with his tongue hanging out, thick and still and yellow, on his green lower lip. Rain drops fell into his open mouth. Then he disappeared with a gentle, sucking sound into the morass, unnoticed except by Friel, who gaped at him in horror. In another moment, all that was left to mark his sojourn on this earth was a series of circular wrinkles in the slime that covered the surface of the quagmire and five orphan children, fathered by him, living with their widowed mother in Canning Town, London: all proudly bearing his name, that of a hero who died in action, fighting for his king and country.

Nobody except Friel took any notice of this hero's death at that moment, and when the bubble at the centre of the series of circles, at the point where his nose had disappeared, burst and vanished, Friel sighed with relief and turned towards the Corporal.

Gunn had taken no notice of the death of Appleby. Again he and the Corporal were face to face as they had been the night before. Now, however, the situation was reversed. Gunn had the Corporal's life, literally, in his hands, as he held him by the wrist. The Corporal, staring in silence at Gunn's face, wore the expression of a cornered fox. Gunn's eyes, avoiding the Corporal's, had a wild look in them. The Corporal's danger had restored his humanity. But the touch of the Corporal's flabby hand excited him unpleasantly. This unpleasant feeling was not articulate. It was like an impression received by a man whose brain is reeling under the first assault of a heavy drunkenness; when words and thoughts stand in a very remote corner of the mind and are scarcely audible or recognisable. This unpleasantness was obviously hatred, but Gunn could not fathom its meaning at that moment. He turned away his face from it in fear, lest his eyes, meeting those of the Corporal, might lead him at once to the disaster that he felt was looming up somewhere in the distance.

They joined two sets of equipment and managed with a great deal of difficulty to pull the Corporal on to the bank. He had behaved like a brave man and a disciplined soldier. He did not relax until they had laid him on the bank. Then, utterly exhausted, he closed his eyes, lay back, drew in a deep breath and became unconscious. The strain on his body, being hauled out, had almost pulled him to pieces. He was covered with terrible slime as sticky as glue. They began to scrape the mud off him.

Gunn, looking at him as he lay on the ground, unconscious and caked in slime, like a Channel swimmer, had another hallucination. He saw the Corporal's body becoming transformed into that of an animal. At once he hurriedly stepped aside, brushed his eyes with his sleeve and then looked wildly at his comrades. Nobody had noticed him. 'God!' he said to himself, 'what's coming over me?'

He moved away from them. All the section was there except Lamont. Gunn went to look for his comrade. He was now trembling. When he got round the corner of the traverse, he halted, looked back furtively and said to himself, 'They'll catch the two of us at it. Sure as God they will!'

He started and listened in awe to the sounds of the words he had uttered to himself, re-echoing in his brain.

'What?' he said to himself. 'What will they catch us at? Trying to escape? I must leave that little devil. He'll get me hung. Where is he now? I'll go and tell him he must chuck it and muck in with the others. We've got to soldier. By God! We've got to stick it.'

Somebody had called out, 'Stretcher-bearers.'

Sergeant Corcoran, followed by Corporal Wallace and Duncan the stretcher-bearer, came up.

'It's Corporal Williams,' said Jennings. 'He fell into a hole.'

'Appleby is ...' began Friel.

The Sergeant brushed him aside before he could finish.

'What cheer, Towny?'

The Sergeant's voice was tender as he knelt beside the Corporal.

The Corporal opened his eyes, shook his head and tried to sit up. 'One of my men, Sergeant,' he stammered, 'Appleby ... in the hole. Fish him out. I lost my rifle.'

'Yes, by God,' said Reilly. 'Appleby is in there.'

The Sergeant jumped to his feet.

'Where?' he cried.

'He's drowned,' said Friel, pointing at the series of circles, that had now almost vanished.

'What?' cried the Sergeant. 'Where is he?'

They explained to him what had happened. They all gazed at the hole.

'I saw him sink,' said Friel. 'He had his tongue stuck out.'

'Then fish him out,' said the Sergeant, in his shrill voice. 'What are you blokes looking at?'

The Corporal sat up.

'I dived in after him,' he said. 'Poor Appleby! Poor bastard!'

The Sergeant threw a piece of wood into the slimy pit. The mud began to suck at the stick at once, like a living thing, dragging it down into its gut.

'It must be fifty feet deep,' said Reilly.

'Napoo,' said the Sergeant.

'Give me a drink,' said the Corporal. 'Haversack, water-bottle, rifle, gas mask and everything gone.'

'Get back, you fellahs,' said the Sergeant.

'Only for Gunn he was done for,' said Friel.

'Stop talking,' said the Sergeant. 'Get on with your work. Jump to it.'

Going back, Shaw met Gunn, who was standing in a bay, staring at the ground.

'What's the matter, mate?' said Shaw.

Gunn started as if struck and turned around. His forehead was deeply furrowed and the whites of his eyes had nearly altogether become stained with blood.

'It's this —— rain,' he said. 'If it doesn't stop I'll ...'

'Keep your hair on, mate,' said Shaw. 'Forget it. Don't worry about being bawled off just now over firing them shots. You'll get away with it. The Sergeant is a decent bloke. His bark is worse than his bite.'

'I'm not worrying about the Sergeant,' said Gunn, in a hoarse voice.

'Everybody has got to bawl off somebody,' said Shaw. 'Forget it.'

Gunn swore and moved on.

Shaw shook his head, shrugged his shoulders and said to himself, 'Gunn is going off his chump. Better be careful.'

Lamont was still gnawing his biscuit when Gunn got back to him.

'What happened?' he said.

'Appleby is gone west,' said Gunn, gazing at the youth with furrowed forehead.

'Really,' said Lamont, opening his lips, pausing, and then continuing to chew.

'What happened to him?' he said, looking vacantly into the distance.

'Eh?' said Gunn.

The youth, still looking vacantly into the distance, stopped chewing for a few moments. Then he continued to chew without repeating the question. He showed no interest in Appleby's death. Concentrating on some purpose or fixed idea, he had become unconscious of his 'immediate' environment. His eyes were unhealthily brilliant.

Gunn scowled at him and moved away. Now he was afraid of Lamont. While Lamont was panic-stricken and acting like a frightened girl, Gunn had merely been irritated with the lad. He had felt superior to him, even though he was being used as a servant and corrupted by ideas of illegal means of escape. Now it was worse, when the lad had suddenly become callous with a strange look in his eyes. He was more like a woman.

The Sergeant came down the trench. Lamont went on chewing his biscuit and gazing into the distance until the Sergeant stopped in front of him. Then he looked at the Sergeant, opened his mouth and assumed a pathetic expression.

'Hey, you!' yelled the Sergeant.

He paused, drew in a deep breath and then, in a low, biting voice, uttered a long oath, which contained five nouns and nine adjectives. Lamont trembled beneath this awesome abuse.

'I'll dance in your guts,' said the Sergeant, 'if you don't wake up. Hop it. Jump. Take his number, Corporal.'

He moved on.

Lamont threw away the bit of biscuit he was chewing.

'Take him, idle,' said the Sergeant, moving away.

The Corporal, even though he was trembling from head to foot as he walked after the Sergeant, at once became rigid when he heard this order. He dived into his tunic pocket for his notebook. His hands were so thickly coated with slime that he could do nothing with them. He called on Friel to take out the notebook and pencil. Friel had also to write down Lamont's name, number and crime report.

Gunn burst out laughing.

'That bloke is going off his knocker,' said Shaw to Jennings.

'What did I tell you blokes?' said Reilly, coming along. 'Not one of us'll come out alive. There's one gone already. Old Appleby. A crummy bloody soldier he was but still ... There's only eight of us left now.'

Gunn laughed again.

They all looked at him.

'It's all a cod,' said Gunn.

'What is a cod?' said the Corporal.

'The whole war is a cod. I just saved you from drowning, and now you're taking my chum's number. Why not take all our numbers, and be done with it, for every crime

71

in the King's Regulations? All our numbers are up, so it doesn't matter.'

The Corporal looked at Gunn viciously. Then he walked past him without speaking.

The men began to mutter.

'It's not bloody well fair,' said Reilly, 'when all is said and done, taking a man's number in the front line for next to nothing. I'm referring to Bill and not to you,' he said to Lamont. 'You bloody little stink, you're always getting somebody into trouble. You're good for nothing.'

'Let the kid alone, Reilly,' muttered Gunn.

The Corporal came back, again fully armed and equipped. The corpse of a man who had been killed in Corporal Tyson's section had been stripped to equip him. He brought a fresh order.

'We're to post sentries and drum up,' he said. 'We're going to advance at eleven o'clock. Pass it along. Who's next for sentry? You, Gunn. It's your turn. The rest can fall out and drum up.'

Gunn, still grinning, turned his face to the hill in front, laid his rifle along the parados and covered the breach with a piece of sacking. Lamont came over to him.

'Say, Bill,' he said. 'Have you got the rations?'

Gunn turned around. Lamont had a mess-tin in his hand.

'What are you going to do?' he said.

'I'm going to make tea,' said Lamont.

'How?' said Gunn, pointing at the sky, from which rain was still pouring. 'What a hope you have!'

'The others are going to try,' said Lamont.

'All right. Take the tea and sugar in my haversack.'

Lamont opened the haversack, took out the packet and closed the sack. Then he whispered, 'What's the matter, Bill?'

The youth's voice was tender. Gunn looked at him. Seeing the boy's beautiful face, with despair in his young eyes and his pale lips drawn tightly together to repress the emotion caused by a sudden memory of his mother, Gunn nearly broke into tears. He wanted to say something kind to the lad, or to take him in his arms and run out of the trench, out of that damned, sodden, rotting place, to green earth and peace. But he turned to his front again without saying anything. And he grinned at the hill which concealed the enemy.

'Will we eat that tin of Maconochie, Bill?' said Lamont. 'I could warm it up on my mess-tin lid.'

'Do what you like,' said Gunn.

'Would you rather I fried the tin of bully?'

Gunn made no reply.

'We have no cheese. The rats bored a hole through my haversack and ate it.'

Gunn turned around and said savagely: 'I told you to put it in your mess-tin, where they couldn't get at it.'

He was now determined to conquer his feeling for the boy, to cease hating the Corporal, to become a good, obedient, thoughtless soldier once more. He must root out the weakness inspired in him by Lamont.

'But I had the cake in my mess-tin,' said Lamont. 'I couldn't let the rats eat the cake that ... she sent me.'

'Oh, blast !...'

Gunn stopped short, on the point of cursing the boy's mother. 'Go on,' he said. 'Do what you like. Go ahead.'

The lad walked away a few yards and then stood still, not knowing how to drum up in the rain without shelter or dry wood. The Corporal, as usual, had seized the only shelter in that part of the trench, a nook formed by the posts of a destroyed dug-out. His mucking-in chum, Shaw, was already getting ready to make tea in the nook, shaving with his jack-knife some pieces of dry wood he had found.

Nearby, Reilly, the other old soldier, stood watching Shaw out of the corner of his eye, while he caressed the drooping ends of his moustache. Friel, who mucked in with Reilly, came up with two barbed wire stakes.

'These what you want?' he asked.

'Do all right, I think,' said Reilly.

He stuck his bayonet into the side of the trench, at a point where the parapet bulged. He stuck a stake of barbed wire into the wall on either side of the bayonet, a little higher up. Then he spread an oil-sheet over the stakes, lacing the ends of the sheet around them. He hung a mess-tin on the bayonet. Then he begged a piece of dry wood from Shaw.

At that moment, McDonald, who had dug a hole in the side of the parapet with his entrenching tool and was now rummaging for his rations, suddenly cried out, with great violence, 'Well, I deserve what I got for letting that bloody fool keep our rations. Now he's gone and drowned himself and they're drowned with him.'

'What are you talking about?' said the Corporal, who sat near Shaw, scraping the mud off his uniform with his jack-knife.

'Appleby,' said McDonald. 'He had our rations.'

'Yes,' said Jennings, in his odd officer's voice. 'He had the whole jolly lot with him.'

'The bloody fool!' said McDonald. 'Now what are we going to do?'

'Serves you right, you savage,' cried Gunn. 'Is that the way you refer to a dead comrade?'

'Look to your front there, Gunn,' said the Corporal.

'God!' thought Gunn, biting his lip. 'He won't give me a chance. He'll make me do it.'

'By Jesus!' said McDonald. 'I'll dig him out of that hole to get my rations.'

'You see,' said Jennings, 'I'm an odd man since my mate went back sick, so I mucked in with Appleby and McDonald. There was a tin of posset belonging to me personally.'

'What about me?' shouted McDonald, his ape-like face writhing with passion. 'There was a sack-full of grub, including three tins of French bully we found in a dug-out on fatigue yesterday. All the bloody trouble I got digging the b— up is gone for nothing. I'm going to get it though.'

He set off towards the traverse where Appleby got drowned.

'Come back, you mad glutton,' said the Corporal. 'I'll give you a drop of tea, if there's any left.'

McDonald came back.

'What's the good of tea?' said McDonald. 'I wish I had eaten that French bully when I got it.'

'Well! You ate four tins of it,' said Reilly. 'Blimme! I saw him digging into it like a savage, sitting beside the stinking corpse. You'd be tied up for duration if an officer saw you. Come here. Give me that dry wood you got, and muck in with us.'

'Get busy, lad,' said Shaw to Lamont. 'Ain't you going to drum up?'

Shaw had already lit a fire under his mess tin. Lamont was standing by watching him.

'He's waiting for his mother to come and do it for him,' said the Corporal. 'You needn't expect me to feed you. I'm not your father.'

Lamont winced at the reference to his mother. Gunn shuddered and ground his teeth, staring at the hill.

'He'll make me do it,' he said.

Now the sound of the Corporal's voice hurt his nerves, like a finger nail being rubbed against a stone.

'Come on, boy,' said Reilly to Lamont. 'Bring your mess tin over here. There's room for it on this bayonet. Chip some slivers. Get out your knife.'

They started a fire under the two mess-tins, with the wood McDonald had foraged.

McDonald, Jennings, Friel and Lamont were now gathered around Reilly, while Shaw and the Corporal sat apart. The Corporal got jealous of Reilly ordering his men about and taking them under his protection.

'I suppose, Reilly,' he said, 'you think you're a hell of a fellow now, being the father of rookies.'

'There he is again,' said Gunn to himself. 'He can let nothing alone.'

'I'm no more a rookie than you are, Corporal,' said McDonald, always eager to take offence. 'Trouble is that you're a rookie as a Corporal. In Corporal Wallace's section ...'

'What's your number?' cried the Corporal, furiously angry.

'Before you came up,' said McDonald. 'You can't crime me for what I didn't say.'

'Eh?' said the Corporal.

'I didn't say it,' said McDonald.

'What didn't you say?' said the Corporal. 'You did say it.'

'What did I say?' said McDonald. 'Ask Reilly if I said it.'

McDonald always got out of an argument by infecting his opponent with the confusion of his own stupidity. His mind had neither a beginning nor an end. It was a circle. The Corporal swore at him and became silent, conscious that he had been put to shame in front of his section, conscious that his men had no respect for him and that they were comparing him unfavourably in their minds and in their conversation with Corporal Wallace.

Corporal Wallace was the most popular N.C.O. in the company. All his men lived in a spirit of complete friendship with him. He got all the intelligent and well-mannered recruits, whereas every 'tough' was ushered into the bombing section. It was the resting place of N.C.O.s who had been reduced to the ranks and of recruits who had to be 'broken in' with an iron hand. In the bombing section men were always being crimed and everybody was at loggerheads with his comrades and with his Corporal. There was a saying in the company: 'Stand to your kits. Here comes one of Corporal Williams' bombers.' Yet every man in the section, except Lamont, wore a ribbon on his tunic.

Suddenly Gunn, on sentry, cried out, 'Christ! Look at the cavalry!'

Everybody jumped up, as excited as if the miracle of

the loaves and fishes was being performed in No Man's Land within their reach; all except Shaw, whose mess-tin was almost boiling.

'Where?' said the Corporal.

'There, on the left. See?'

'I declare to God they are,' said Reilly. 'Horses.'

'Never see horses before?' said Shaw, puffing at his fire.

'But what on earth are they doing here?' said Jennings.

'God only knows!' said Reilly. 'Probably a circus going to start. The war mustn't be paying, so they're going to turn it into a circus.'

'They must be circus horses,' said Friel, 'to be able to come up over the duck-boards.'

They all gaped in wonder at the horses, which looked like skeletons, dimly outlined against the horizon on the left, with their cloaked riders stooping forward from the rain. They moved very slowly in a line, staggering through shell holes, slipping in the mud and rearing.

'Can you beat that for lunacy?' said the Corporal. 'What crazy fool sent those horses up here?'

'Oh! Some mad fool,' said Reilly. 'Pay no heed to anything you see happening in this war. Ha! Now they'll get it.'

There was a rattle of machine-gunfire. A rider threw up his hands. His mount reared and shook its head, pawing the air with one fore-leg, while the other leg hung limply. Then both rider and horse disappeared, falling backwards into the mud. The other horses turned and tried to gallop back. It was impossible for them to gallop. They all seemed to have their spines injured by the way they sprawled, with their legs spread out. Several of them got hit and came down. The others disappeared. The machine-gun ceased fire.

'Fine bloody polo game that was,' said Jennings.

'Jerry is there yet all right,' said the Corporal. 'The war is not over.'

'Hurrah!' said Shaw. 'She's on the boil, Corporal.'

'Warm the tin of pork an' beans,' said the Corporal. 'Much rooty left?'

'Curse and blast it!' said Reilly, rushing back to his mess-tin. 'The fire is gone out while we were looking at those horses. Come on, lads. Chips. Chips.'

Jennings, McDonald, Lamont and Reilly gathered around the tiny fire trying to restore it to life. The Corporal and Shaw began to eat their breakfast. Gunn, on sentry, smelt the Corporal's breakfast and became terribly excited. He could hear the Corporal making noises as he ate.

Looking around, he saw the Corporal stuffing bread, pork, beans and tea into his mouth with great rapidity, and then swallowing them all ravenously and filling his mouth afresh with bread, pork, beans and tea, before the first mouthful had gone down his throat.

'Christ! How I hate him!' said Gunn to himself, as he turned to his front.

Then he became aware of his own body, with that painfully vivid consciousness which is nearly always present in a sensitive, intelligent being and leads to refinement of thought and conduct, but which is almost entirely alien to a strong, stupid person. When it strikes the latter it causes a dangerous ferment that leads invariably to ill-considered violence.

Gunn felt something, actually alive, leaping against his

ribs and against the walls of his stomach, struggling to break forth.

'Look out! Oh, God Almighty!'

It was Reilly who had shouted. In their excitement, the men feeding the fire under the mess-tins had paid no attention to the rain-water that was gathering on the oil-sheet overhead. The oil-sheet had sagged down in the middle, laden with water. Now it fell, dragging the stakes and the bayonet with it. The mess-tins overturned. There was a sizzling sound and an acrid smell of wet ashes. McDonald's hand was burned as he held fresh slivers to the flames.

All gaped. The Corporal laughed.

'Now,' he cried, taunting Reilly. 'What price old soldiers?'

Reilly, undefeated, shrugged his shoulders and said, 'Could I use your fire, '20?'

'No time now,' said the Corporal. 'Get your rifles clean.'

Gunn's eyes glittered.

The others looked at one another, speechless with misery. This spilling of two quarts of hot water was a greater disaster to each of them than the loss of an eye. It was the last straw in the load of misery that overwhelmed them.

A look of despair came into their eyes. Gunn, looking from one to the other of them, felt a black joy at the despair in their eyes. It fortified his growing purpose.

'I hate him! I hate him,' he repeated.

His mind had now taken the shape of a glass ball, in the interior of which there are pictures. The ball expanded and contracted. Expanded, it contained a picture of the whole army, from the Commander-in-Chief with his staff, right down the ranks of Authority, to the great nameless, numbered multitude of men like himself, who lay hungry and wet and covered with mud in holes, DOOMED TO DIE. Contracted, he saw in it only the Corporal and himself.

The Corporal was a grinning brute. He himself was a savage man with a club.

Lamont came over and whispered, 'Might as well have a piece of this cake, Bill. '

Gunn swallowed a lump in his throat, looked into the youth's DEAD eyes, and muttered tenderly, 'Stick to me, kid. And, by God! If anything happens to you ... D'ye hear?'

Chapter Six

The rain ceased about ten o'clock. The sky grew clear. The battle front was still silent. The men caught sight of a green slope, afar off on the left, beyond a hollow.

'Look,' said Jennings, 'there's grass there. Astonishing.'

With the exception of Lamont, none of them had seen a blade of grass for five months.

'By Christ!' said Reilly, 'the next thing we'll see is a woman.'

They became quite cheerful at the sight of green grass.

'Listen!' cried McDonald, 'that's a bird singing.'

'Yes!' said Friel. 'It's a lark. My God! That's open country out there. That's the end of the desert.'

They all looked at the green grass and listened to the lark singing. The sky was becoming blue and clear. Was the nightmare over? Was peace coming?

That most demoralising thought brought fever to their blood.

Then Reilly brought them back to gloomy reality by saying, 'That's a bad sign. We're for it, lads. It's unlucky to hear a bird singing in No Man's Land.'

Now their faces became drawn and their eyes narrowed as they listened to the eerie singing of the lark in No Man's Land.

'There are Jerries moving up that slope,' said Gunn. 'Where's our bloody artillery?'

'They're on the run,' said the Corporal.

'Like hell they are,' said Reilly. 'That's a gun they are dragging. They're going to pitch their tents there on dry land. I see their idea.'

'What?' said McDonald.

'Why!' said Reilly, 'they'll get us to follow them over this mud. It's a good place for a graveyard. Cheap. Look how Appleby went down. We're done for.'

'Ha!' said Gunn.

A sharp boom came from the rear, followed by another and still another. Overhead, three shells passed whining and burst with a loud crash in the green field where the enemy was moving. The earth spouted up in three fountains where they fell.

'See them run!' cried the Corporal. 'Ha! that got them. See the stretcher-bearers, coming up. Come on, gunners. Give it to the bastards.'

Their faces shone with excitement as the guns began to fire continuously. In spite of their exhaustion, they felt that this tremendous booming in their rear and the huge projectiles that went whining over their heads towards the enemy were an expression of their own power. Like skinny consumptives who are carried away by the thunder of Nietzsche's poetry into a belief in the superman, these hapless wretches at that moment almost believed that the thunder was issuing from their own mouths.

They were hysterical with hunger, wet, want of sleep, lice, terror of death.

They moved about restlessly. Their eyes assumed a tense, fierce expression. They attained a grotesque dignity. They fingered their weapons. Their monster was belching fire. Soon he would thrust forth his claws, thousands of little men, covered with mud, at the enemy.

Gunn, listening to the artillery, was even more excited than the others. Their sound exalted into ecstasy the blood lust that was growing in him.

Chapter Seven

Exactly at eleven o'clock, when the thunder of the guns had reached its climax, two thousand, four hundred and forty-five men stepped out of their holes and walked into No Man's Land towards the enemy. They advanced in artillery formation, by sections.

This time, only seven men went over the top with Corporal Williams. They were gathered about him in a bunch and he looked like the leader of a primitive band of nomads, driven from their hole by rain, hunger, disease or vermin, seeking a better hole. On either side, other Corporals advanced with similar groups. There was no excitement, no haste, no grandeur, no drums, no banners, no gleaming weapons, no plumes, no terrifying devices, no shouting of war-maddened warriors; just little crowds of dirty, stooping men, with ugly steel hats, gas masks, bags of bombs.

A miserable, heatless sun now shone in the sky. The earth seemed a void, barren of life, the crater of a dead world; and the thunder of the guns was no longer romantically awe-inspiring. The crash of their bursting had become barren of power in their ears.

Suddenly, when they had advanced three hundred yards, the enemy opened fire with his artillery. Shells began to fall in front of them. Instinctively, they gathered closer together and shuddered. Their steps became more brisk. Not a word was spoken. The shells fell more thickly. They seemed to be alive, hissing as they swooped through the air. Yet when they burst, they became almost impotent, smothered by the slime.

They reached the slope of the hill and began to ascend. Now machine-guns opened fire to the left. They could see the hollow beyond the hill and afar off, green fields, stumps of trees, ruined houses, walls, roads, black railway lines. But there was no sign of an enemy; just flashes of fire spotting the earth, which was a black crater, scarred with holes, littered with wreckage, coated with oozing slime.

Above the roar of the artillery and the rattle of machine-guns, their anxious ears caught the moaning of wounded men. The signal came: 'Take cover.' 'Down. Down.'

Corporal Williams and his seven men threw themselves on the ground at once and lay still, hugging the mud, unconscious now of hunger, thirst, cold, wet, lice and other miseries, all except one, the misery of death. As still as rabbits and with the fixed eyes of terrified rabbits, they lay flat, while the gigantic missiles whined and burst about them, covering them with a spray of mud. They were under cover from bullets, lying in a crater formed by several shell holes that had been converted into one hole by other shells. There was a roar above their heads, as if the earth had burst and was flying about in clashing fragments, rebursting, revolving. The drums of their ears could not differentiate between sounds. They were no longer afraid. They no longer thought. They had lost individual consciousness. They had ceased to be human.

Then a man came running across from the right, threw himself down into their hole and called in a voice that startled them by its stern fearlessness, 'Corporal Williams!'

It was the Platoon Sergeant. They all raised their heads and started at him in amazement, because he had retained the power of speech and of individual consciousness. He pointed towards the front and yelled something into the Corporal's ear. There was a clod of blood-stained mud or human flesh on his moustache under his nose. Then he jumped to his feet and ran crouching to the right.

The Corporal shouted to his men, 'Come on, lads. We're to dig in there in front. Get ready.'

They again became afraid at the realisation that they had to rise from the mud and become alive, in order to guide their bodies towards a place somewhere in front, where they had to dig, exposed to this shower of hot iron.

'It's a massacre,' whined Jennings.

'Get ready, lads ,' said the Corporal.

Suddenly, Lamont, who lay beside Gunn, jumped to his feet and, dropping his rifle, tried to run out of the hole towards the enemy.

Gunn seized him and hauled him back.

'Wait for it,' shouted the Corporal, in his excitement not understanding the nature of Lamont's movements.

'Now,' he shouted.

They all jumped up and ran forward. Gunn thrust his rifle into Lamont's hand. Then he seized him by the scruff of the neck and dragged him along. The Corporal, running in front, threw himself down. They all followed, dropping around him in a row. They now lay on exposed ground, which offered only a few inches of cover.

'Dig,' cried the Corporal.

'How are we to dig into this?' yelled McDonald in an insane voice, as he thrust his fingers into the slime and then pulled them forth, webbed, as from a cake of kneaded flour.

Now they all babbled.

'What's the good of entrenching tools here?' cried Friel.

'Dig in,' yelled the Corporal.

They got out their entrenching tools and began to dig.

'No use,' said Gunn, savagely driving his tool into the mud. 'It's putty.'

'Dig, you bastards!' screamed the Corporal.

Like idiots, they all began to tear at the mud, without making the slightest impression on the ground. It was a mass of sticky slime. But they worked furiously, without thought, without hope of achieving anything, merely obeying the order to drive their tools into the earth and to pull them forth again.

Lamont struck the ground once feebly with his tool and then hauled at it with both hands trying to draw it forth. His exhausted muscles were unable for the effort. With the handle in his hand, he stared at the ground and shuddered.

Gunn drove his elbow into the boy's side and yelled, 'Keep down. Make cover for yourself.'

Lamont gasped and threw himself against Friel, who was digging on the other side of him. He tried to crawl under Friel's body. Friel swore, raised himself on his knees and then seized Lamont to push him away. Lamont crawled over to Gunn. As Friel was lying down again to dig, he made a loud sound in his nostrils and then grunted. He fell prone, doubled up at once and grasped his stomach with both hands.

He had been shot six times through the stomach. He began to moan.

Just then a shell burst immediately behind them. They all lay flat, while the mud dislodged by the shell came falling down. Then they heard Friel moaning.

'Who's that?' cried the Corporal, raising his head.

He looked all round him and saw two things that interested him. One was Friel, lying on his face, writhing, grasping his stomach with his hands. The other was men running back on all sides. Somebody, far back, was signalling, giving the order to retire.

'Retire,' cried the Corporal. 'Get out of it.'

Lamont jumped up first and ran back like a deer. As McDonald was about to follow, he saw Friel and stooped to pick him up.

'Leave him to me,' said Reilly. 'Run.'

'Shouldn't we open rapid fire,' said Shaw, 'while Friel is carried back?'

'There are no orders to fire,' said the Corporal.

'Jesus!' said Reilly. 'What a bloody circus!'

Gunn and Reilly dragged Friel back into a shell hole.

The others raced back, scattering into various shell holes. Here it was quiet. They were under cover from machine-gunfire, sheltered by the hill. The shells were all dropping in front, exactly where they had been ordered to dig in by the officers in charge.

Gunn and Reilly cut open Friel's greatcoat and tunic. He was bleeding terribly. The Corporal dashed over from the shell hole into which he had dropped. Everybody was calling for stretcher-bearers. Men in other shell holes were also calling for stretcher-bearers. Nobody came. They tried to bandage the wound, but it was impossible to do so, as the stomach seemed to be full of holes. On account of the filthy state of their hands and their utter weariness, they only added to the poor wretch's agony without helping him.

'Where is the dressing station?' said Reilly. 'We can do nothing with him. He's bleeding internally. His guts are smashed.'

'Where is the dressing station?' said the Corporal. 'Eh?'

Nobody knew where anything was. They just gaped at one another.

'Come on,' said Reilly. 'Put him on my back. I'll carry him.'

As soon as they tried to lift him, Friel uttered a horrible moan and clawed at them. Then he began to wriggle and a great gush of blood issued from his stomach through the field bandages they had placed on it. His face contorted. He bared his teeth, opened his mouth and just when he was going to close it, Reilly thrust the handle of his jack-knife between the teeth. His jaws closed with a snap; he shivered, and strange gurgling noises issued from his throat.

'Stretcher-bearers, for Christ's sake!' cried Gunn.

Friel began to make sounds like a dummy, a loutish mumbling. He threw out his right leg and tapped the ground violently with his heel. Then he shook all over and lay still, all except his chest, which rose and fell slowly, at long intervals, causing a rumble in his throat. Another stream of blood gushed forth, covering Reilly's hand.

Reilly took away the bloody hand which he had placed on the torn stomach to press in the bandages. 'Good-bye, lad. Cheerio!' he said.

Gunn got to his feet, stared angrily at the Corporal and began to curse.

'What did you say?' said the Corporal.

Gunn raised his hand, muttered something and sat down, looking at the ground gloomily.

The Corporal, paying no heed to him, leaned over the side of the hole and yelled, 'Keep your heads down! Stretcher-bearers!'

Shells were beginning to fall around. The enemy was getting the range again. Friel was now motionless.

'It's too late now,' said Reilly. 'He's gone West.'

The jack-knife was still in Friel's mouth. Reilly forced open the jaws and pulled it out. The jaws would not close again.

No. 9087 Private Michael Friel, formerly a constable in the Royal Irish Constabulary, had died from haemorrhage, following numerous gun-shot wounds in the abdomen, received in action. He left three mistresses, resident in Dublin, London and Liverpool.

'Where's Lamont?' said Gunn, jumping to his feet.

He ran out of the hole, threw himself on the ground while a shell burst and then ran on again, shouting, 'Hey! Louis! Where are you?'

McDonald stuck his head out of a hole and cried, 'He's here.'

He ducked again at once. Gunn entered that hole. Lamont was sitting at the bottom, doubled up. McDonald was cutting open a tin of bully beef. He stopped when Gunn looked at him. Gunn glanced at Lamont and the turned to McDonald.

'Where did you get the bully?' he said. 'You took it from the kid.'

'Yer a liar, I didn't,' said McDonald. 'It's out of my ...'

He paused and looked around him furtively. He was eating his iron rations.

Gunn raised Lamont's head. The boy was deadly pale. He tried to smile and then drew in his breath through his teeth. Gunn dropped the lad's head.

'Give us a bit,' he said to McDonald.

He now felt terribly hungry.

'Eat your own rations,' said McDonald, ravenously devouring lumps of meat that he hauled out of the tin with his knife.

Suddenly Gunn, who had been only semi-conscious from the moment that he stepped out of the enemy's front line trench, began to think once more.

A crowd of images and words rushed into his brain. He covered his eyes with his hands, trying to conceal himself from the images. Then a voice within him began to repeat: 'Kill him! Kill him! Kill him!'

He shuddered, took away his hands from his eyes, looked at Lamont and began to tap the boy on the back, making a sucking noise in the corner of his cheek, like a man making friends with a dog.

'Hey!' said McDonald. 'What are you doing?'

Gunn looked up.

McDonald threw away the remains of his bully beef, stood up and cried out in a terrified voice, 'Hey! Corporal!'

'Sit down,' muttered Gunn, 'or I'll run my bayonet through ye.'

McDonald ran out of the hole, leaving his rifle. He dived into the hole where Corporal Williams was. Two stretcher-bearers had now arrived. They were taking away Friel's corpse.

'Gunn is gone mad,' said McDonald.

'You're daft, yourself, you fool,' said the Corporal. 'What's he trying on? That's an old dodge.'

'Come and see him,' said McDonald. 'He threatened to bayonet me.'

Now the enemy shell-fire had ceased again. Men were standing up in their holes on all sides, looking about them. The Corporal, Reilly and McDonald walked across to the hole where McDonald had been.

'Better be careful, Corporal,' said Reilly. 'If he's off his chump ...'

'Don't you worry,' said the Corporal.

Shaw and Jennings were standing up in another hole father away.

'Is Friel badly hurt?' said Shaw.

'Gone West,' said Reilly.

'What's the ticket now then?' said Shaw. 'Where are you off to?'

The Corporal, getting afraid of Gunn as he approached, signalled to Shaw, pointing to the hole where Gunn lay.

'What's up?' cried Jennings.

Shaw got out of his hole, signalling to Jennings to follow him. They thus approached Gunn from both sides, as if ambushing an enemy, with their rifles at the high port. They arrived all together on the banks of the hole. They found Gunn sitting on his heels, ravenously devouring the remains of McDonald's bully beef. He looked up at them in surprise. His face looked calm, showing nothing more strange than the rather disgusting expression of a half-starved man devouring food.

'What are you doing there?' said the Corporal.

Lamont looked up, roused by the Corporal's voice. Gunn dropped the bully beef tin and rubbed his hands along his thighs. He remained silent.

'He's eaten my bully,' said McDonald, jumping down into the hole.

Gunn looked from man to man, blinking.

'I thought you didn't want any more of it,' he said to McDonald. 'You threw it away.'

'Did you threaten to bayonet McDonald, Gunn?' said the Corporal.

'I?' said Gunn. 'Who said so?'

McDonald had picked up the tin and looked into it. It was empty. 'He's finished it,' he cried in rage. 'My iron rations.'

'Your what?' cried the Corporal, forgetting Gunn in the excitement of having discovered a serious crime to enter into his notebook. 'You ate your iron rations?'

McDonald waved his hands. His ape-like face wrinkled. His teeth chattered. He could think of no excuse to offer for the crime which his stupidity and gluttony had exposed.

'Speak up!' cried the Corporal, jumping down into the hole.

McDonald, almost in tears, began to explain how 'the bloody fool, Appleby, went and drowned himself, with all our rations'.

'What's your number?' said the Corporal.

Gunn looked up and saw Shaw whispering to Reilly. He knew they were talking about him. He also knew that they thought he was mad and that they were discussing the best thing to do with him. And he suddenly became aware of a great cunning in himself. He became conscious of it, *actually* saw it in his mind (at least, he imagined he saw it, which amounted to the same thing). In a flash, he told himself that he must deceive them, for now at all costs he must avoid being sent back from the line until he had done what he intended to do.

Speaking quite coldly, much more coolly than anybody else in the hole, he said to Shaw, 'Give us a smoke, '20. I know you have a packet.'

Shaw looked at him in surprise.

'Come on, mate,' said Gunn, smiling and showing a set of flashing white teeth, which contrasted strangely with his coarse face. The whiteness of his teeth made his face look cunningly evil at that moment, instead of stupid, as it had been until then.

His face was now 'strange' and inhuman.

Shaw came down into the hole, and gave him a piece of cigarette. Reilly and Jennings also came down into the hole. Now the whole section was there, sitting close together, all hysterical with fear, exhaustion and shock, except Gunn who was mad.

The Corporal had forgotten to 'crime' McDonald for his offence. He was too hysterical and exhausted to execute a simple purpose. McDonald was scraping out the tin of bully beef. Lamont, indifferent to his environment, stared into the distance. The Corporal, suddenly aware of his utter exhaustion, covered his face with his hands and yawned. Reilly and Shaw, being old soldiers and properly trained, sat motionless, without thought, just conserving their life; which is the only proper occupation of a soldier not fulfilling an order. Jennings scratched himself with one hand and with the other searched his pockets for the butt of a cigarette. Gunn's eyes glittered.

Chapter Eight

While they were sitting idle in this fashion in the hole, the Sergeant appeared. He was walking casually, with his rifle at the trail. He seemed to be in a great humour.

'Come out of your holes, bombers,' he said. 'Jerry is gone again.'

They all looked up quickly and made a move to get on their feet, startled by the Sergeant's appearance. A soldier is always terrified when caught sitting in idleness by a superior; even when he is entitled to sit in idleness. But the Sergeant was in such good humour that he forgot to abuse them for sitting idly in their hole during an engagement.

'Is he retiring?' said the Corporal. 'That true, Sergeant?'

'Yes,' said the Sergeant. 'The war is all over now bar the shouting.'

The men uttered exclamations of delight. A look of awe came into their faces.

'Are we going after him, Sarg?' said the Corporal.

'Not just yet,' said the Sergeant. 'Can't bring up the guns over this blasted mud. That's what the delay is about. We're to wait here till dark and try to bring up the rations. Nobody exactly knows what's on. He retired suddenly.'

Then he changed his tone, and said, gloomily, 'Looks as if we're going to be in the line for keeps.'

Now he spoke from his heart. Before, he had spoken as a Sergeant, whose duty it was to cheer the men with good news and restore their morale, which had been sapped by this ridiculous operation in the mud, sapped by lice, by mud, by rain, by hunger, by lack of faith in the wisdom of 'the blokes in the rear'.

But the men believed his lies and paid no attention to his truth. The Corporal even forgot to mention the death of Friel in his excitement. As the Sergeant walked away, the Corporal called after him, 'Are we to wait here, Sergeant?'

'Yes,' said the Sergeant. 'Wait there.'

Now a hysteria of joy, in direct reaction to their recent hysteria of melancholy, overtook these seven men; overtook even Lamont, whose eyes lost their fixity and began to blink, like a young girl awaking from a swoon.

As if they said to themselves, 'Hello! He's retiring. Shells are not falling. We are certain of remaining alive for another few hours. Let's make the most of them.'

The Corporal jumped out of the hole, put his rifle on his shoulder and swaggered about, saying, 'I told you blokes the war was over. I felt it in the air. Fritz is done for. He can't stand up to it. If we could get up the artillery, now, we'd drive him to Berlin in a week. Keep him going. That's all we need.'

He sat down and tightened his puttees.

'Jesus!' said McDonald, forgetting the crime of having

eaten his iron rations through excess of hunger and the disastrous death of Appleby, who had incontinently got drowned while carrying his comrades' rations. 'I wouldn't mind a scrap tonight. I hope they'll send us on a bombing raid. Jerry is sure to leave a lot of grub behind on his retreat.'

Reilly rubbed together his two hands, which were covered with the gore that had flown from Friel's lacerated belly. 'You can have his grub,' he chuckled. 'I'd like to get a cart-load of them new field glasses and stuff that the Jerry officers have.'

'Be all right getting into a good billet,' said Shaw, licking his lips. 'Wouldn't say no to a nice fat German wench.'

Gunn kept smiling, looking from face to face.

'There'll never be another war,' said Jennings. 'You'll never get fellows to go on a stunt like this again. By Jove! I'll clear out to the South Sea Islands as soon as I get home. Lie all day in the sun, with native women feeding me on bananas. To hell with civilisation.'

'When do you think we'll get home?' said Lamont.

'Home?' said the Corporal. 'Eh?'

The word *home* silenced their babbling. It reminded them of an unattainable reality which the Sergeant's lies could not bring within reach of their credulous minds. As when the sum emerges suddenly from dark clouds on a spring day, shines for a few moments, making the earth gay and beautiful and then is covered again, leaving the day still gloomier, so they relapsed into despair. At once their faces mirrored their despair.

Then Gunn burst forth, 'It's all a cod. I know damn well it's a cod. Jerry is not retiring. They're only saying that to put us in a good humour, after making a hash of the whole thing. What do they take us for?'

They all looked at him and remembered that a few minutes before he had startled them by his queerness. Lamont's eyes again became fixed. The Corporal, sitting above the hole, assumed his habitual expression of cunning and suspicion.

'Who do you think you are?' he said. 'If you were running the war it would be over long ago, wouldn't it? Eh?'

Gunn turned towards the Corporal and said in a sombre voice, 'If I were running this war, in any case, Appleby and Friel'd be alive now. These two men have been murdered.'

The Corporal opened his mouth to say something, but kept silent. He began to bob his head on his thin neck and he rolled the tape of his puttee round and round his leg with great energy. Then he said: 'What's it got to do with you? Your business is to obey orders and keep your mouth shut. You better be careful, my lad. Understand?'

He got to his feet, told the men not to move and walked away, going in the direction of Corporal Wallace. Gunn stood up and looked around him. Men were moving about in all directions. They resembled a swarm of ants that have been dislodged and are dashing about, seemingly without guidance, trying to restore order. Gunn saw the Sergeant-Major and the Company Commander in the distance. They were walking back towards the rear, followed by their servants, as calm and as tidy as if they were going on a stroll. They irritated him. He cursed at them, and sat down again.

'Listen, mate,' said Shaw to him. 'You better be careful what you say. You might get yourself into trouble. In the army, once they get their knife in you, they rub it in. You'll be blamed for everything. There's no use trying to beat them.'

'I don't give a damn,' said Gunn, fiercely. 'Since I came out here, I've done my bit. I've soldiered and I've never said a word, except what a man might say when he has his rag out. But I'm fed up with it. They're not going to put the wind up me. I'll not let him walk on me. He's always picking at me and my mate. I know why. Because Monty wouldn't share his parcels with him. I tell you this is a lousy mob.'

'The mob is all right, mate,' said Shaw.

Gunn stared at the old soldier.

'Aw!' he said. 'You're only a slave. You think because you're an old soldier you're something. But you're only a slave. A bloody machine. Any mule could be trained to do what you can do. '

'Watch out, boy,' said Shaw, his bronzed face getting redder.

'Chuck it, lads,' said Reilly.

'Let him alone, Reilly,' said Gunn. 'I'll soon settle his hash.'

Shaw winced and veins stood out on his sturdy neck; but he controlled himself and turned away. His sense of discipline gained mastery over his temper.

Gunn was now in the full tide of his fury.

'Up there they've got it,' he said, tapping his forehead. 'They can do what they like with us. Chucking us out of our post last night, without giving a damn what happened

101

to us. All day they have us mucking about. What for? Just for fun. Same way with those poor bloody horses they sent up. What for? They don't know. They don't care. They're full of rum. By Christ! Appleby and Friel don't care either. They're dead now. I wouldn't mind if they died fighting. But there hasn't been a shot fired. Not a bloody shot.'

'Except the shots you fired,' said Reilly, who had been listening to Gunn's outburst with a curious expression of boredom and indifference on his face. 'Take my tip for it. If you start thinking you'll gain nothing by it. It's dangerous work. All the jails at home are full of people who started to think and were caught in the act. There's a law against it.'

'You turn everything into a joke, Reilly,' said Gunn.

'Why not?' said Reilly.

'Oh! Blast you,' said Gunn. 'Blast the lot of you. Give me that tin of Maconochie, Louis.'

Suddenly a voice began to sing in the distance, faintly, in a tone that was excruciatingly melancholy:—

> *I want to go home,*
> *I want to go home.*
> *I don't want to go to the trenches no more*
> *Where whizz-bangs always do roar.*
> *Take me over the sea,*
> *Where the Alleymand can't get at me.*
> *Oh! My! I don't want to die.*
> *I want to go home.*

Their heads drooped, listening to the dreary song, that agonising cry of doomed men, waiting for death.

Chapter Eight

The Corporal came back, and said, 'Two men for a fatigue party. We're going to dig in there in front. Jump to it, Gunn. You too, McDonald. Picks and shovels coming up.'

Gunn jumped up and swore.

'Could I loose a button, Corporal?' said Jennings.

Chapter Nine

At three o'clock an order came that they were to advance and dig a hole on the far side of the hill. Corporal Williams again set forth with his men. Now there's only seven souls in the section.

Not a shot was fired as they trudged through the mud. When they crossed the brow of the hill there was no sign of the enemy anywhere. They marched in silence, slowly, without interest. Now they were too bored to notice where they were going or to look around them. They had become merely figures, that moved when ordered, halted when ordered, lay down when ordered and dug when ordered. The silence was a drug. When they had covered the required distance the Corporal ordered them to halt. He then walked about, choosing the best place to dig. After consultation with Reilly and Shaw he chose a spot and ordered them to dig. They spread out in a line and seized their tools.

But they had no sooner begun to dig than the enemy opened fire on them. It seemed as if the cunning fellow were playing a game with them, enticing them into a trap, firing at them when they came to a spot on which his weapons were trained, and then retiring when he had killed a few of them.

They lay flat on the ground while bullets whizzed over their heads. Then the firing stopped. They waited. Corporal Williams raised his steel hat on a shovel. Nobody fired at it.

'Snipers,' he said. 'Come on. Dig.'

'Why not open fire on the bastards?' said Reilly.

'There are orders not to waste ammunition,' said the Corporal. 'We may need all we have tonight. Can't get any up.'

'God! What a life!' said Jennings.

They began to dig rapidly. An enemy machine-gun opened fire on Corporal Wallace's section, which was digging a hole on the right.

'Why the hell don't they use their Lewis gun?' said Gunn. 'Is this supposed to be a funny joke?'

'Shut your trap,' said the Corporal. 'Dig in.'

'This is a funny engagement,' said Jennings. 'It should be set to music and produced as a comic opera.'

'Dig in and stop talking,' said the Corporal. 'Christ!'

A shower of rifle grenades came whining through the air, almost on top of them. They lay flat while the grenades burst. Nobody was hit.

'He's out there somewhere,' said Reilly, with his face in the mud. 'There's a nest of them near here somewhere.'

'Come on, lads,' said the Corporal. 'Dig in.'

Again they began to dig furiously. Here the ground was firmer. After they had removed the muddy crust of the earth, their tools worked efficiently.

After a few minutes, Jennings ceased to dig, and called

out, 'Say, Corporal, I have to fall out for a moment.'

'What's the matter with you? Keep your head down or you'll lose it.'

'I simply can't wait another minute,' said Jennings.

Forthwith he unfastened his uniform and crouched like a cat on the little hole he had scraped in the mud.

'Lie down,' said McDonald, who was beside Jennings. 'See here, Corporal, he'll draw fire on us.'

'I simply can't wait,' whimpered Jennings.

'Knock him down,' cried the Corporal. 'What's your number, Jennings?'

A rifle grenade whizzed and burst right in front of the post. At the same time a machine-gun opened fire on them. They lay flat. Jennings fell forward and grunted. The machine-gun stopped firing.

'I say, fellows,' said Jennings in a strange tone. 'I say, you chaps. Look! Do look!'

'What?' cried McDonald, raising his head. 'What are you ...? Holy jumping son of ... Look at him!'

'Say, Mac,' said Jennings, holding out his right arm, 'do you think I'm wounded? Am I cut? Do you see any blood?'

He had thrown up his right arm to shield his face when the grenade burst. It was hanging by a strip of skin within the sleeve of his greatcoat, shattered below the elbow. The sleeve of his coat had been ripped to the shoulder. His hand hung incongruously downwards as he held up his arm. Blood was pouring from the wound in a full stream. His sleeve was becoming dark as the blood soaked through the cloth. His trousers and underwear had fallen down about his heels. His thighs, as thin and

106

frayed as those of an old man, were spattered with blood. His eyeballs protruded like those of a rabbit whose neck has been smartly broken. Froth bubbled on his lips as he babbled.

'Lie down, blast you!' cried the Corporal, crawling over on his belly. 'Cut that bloody sleeve, Crap. Off with his puttees.'

'Oh! I see,' whimpered Jennings. 'I'm really wounded. I do hope it's not serious. I'm bleeding. By Jove!'

'Bloody artery is cut,' said the Corporal. 'Off with his puttees. Something to burn it ... quick. Stop talking, blast you!'

They threw Jennings on the ground with violence, as he insisted on trying to stand up. They had no means of treating such a wound properly, so they tied puttees about his arm and lashed it double; but still the blood gushed forth. Jennings began to rave. His face became an extraordinary colour. Already his uninjured hand looked like the hand of a corpse. He could not hold his hand steady on his neck. At last, Shaw was detailed to drag him back over the brow of the hill, while McDonald hurried back to call the stretcher-bearers.

'That is three,' said Reilly in a gloomy voice after they had gone. 'What did I tell you? Not one of us'll come out alive.'

'He's got a blighty one, anyway,' said Lamont. 'Wish I had.'

'Shut up, you bloody little ferret,' said the Corporal, wiping Jennings' blood off his hands onto his greatcoat. 'Wish you had gone instead of him. You haven't dug an inch. Get on with your work.'

'That's not a blighty one,' said Reilly. 'He'll never reach the dressing station alive.'

Drrrr. The machine spattered its bullets through the air to the left of them.

'The bastard is firing on the wounded,' cried Gunn. 'By Christ! Somebody is going to pay for this.'

He dug furiously.

'I'm under cover now,' said Reilly. 'What about a rest, Corporal?'

'Dig,' said the Corporal. 'We're not digging for cover. We're making a post.'

They went on digging. After a while, Shaw and McDonald dashed up and threw themselves into the hole, followed by a shower of bullets.

'He got another packet as I was taking him back,' said Shaw. 'Right through the heart, I think. He's gone West.'

'Did you hand him over?' said the Corporal.

'Yes,' said McDonald. 'I got the stretcher-bearers. There's been a lot hit in No. 4 Platoon. It is just like old Jennings. He was always getting taken short at the wrong time. Too much beer.'

'Stop talking,' said the Corporal. 'Dig.'

'We're all for it,' said Reilly, gloomily.

'I wish it hit me instead,' said Lamont, plaintively.

Gunn seized the boy roughly by the arm and whispered in his ear, 'If anything happens to you, kid, they can watch out for themselves. I'll ...'

'Stop talking, Gunn,' said the Corporal, 'Dig.'

They continued to dig. Now the hole was over three feet deep in places. It began to grow dark. Utterly exhausted, they began to pause for breath, one after the other. The Corporal, himself exhausted, urged them back to work again. Now they could only scoop out a few ounces of clay at a time, and their hands moved with the slowness of snails.

Then Lamont dropped his shovel and lay down.

'Get up and dig,' whispered the Corporal, hoarsely.

Lamont did not move. McDonald lay down. Shaw sighed, sat down and dropped his head on his chest. Reilly swore and fell forward on his pick. The Corporal sat down and dropped his head on his right shoulder, mumbling, 'We've got to dig down deeper ... deeper ... we got to ... dig.'

He spoke like a drunken man. Gunn laughed aloud, sat down, folded his arms on his chest and began to strike his teeth together. Reilly began to titter.

'What's the joke?' muttered the Corporal.

Lamont began to snore.

'I'll bet any man five francs,' said Reilly, 'that we'll be told to move on out of here in a minute. The whole idea is to wander around in this mud, scratching. Nothing to do but scrape up mud. Dig, dig, dig. Scratch, scratch.'

'Ha!' said Gunn, 'I see it now.'

'What?' said the Corporal, without looking at him.

Gunn started and wiped his face on his sleeve. He looked at the Corporal. Then he uttered an exclamation and leaned back with outstretched hands, horrified. There was a blur before his eyes and through the blur he saw the Corporal, not in his human shape, but transformed into a hairy brute. He wiped his eyes fiercely and looked again. He stopped breathing with terror. Instead of the Corporal he saw an uncouth animal, like a gorilla, crouching in sleep. He shook Reilly who sat next to him.

'Hey! Hey!' he whispered. 'Wake up, Reilly.'

'What is it?' said Reilly, slowly raising his head.

As soon as Reilly spoke, the blur vanished from before Gunn's eyes, and he saw the Corporal in his human shape. He sighed with relief.

'Eh?' said Reilly. 'What did you say, Bill?'

'I said to wake up,' cried Gunn in a loud voice. 'Don't all go to sleep here.'

He was trembling and the soles of his feet itched. Now his head seemed to be a heavy weight that lay on his neck.

McDonald began to snore.

'Wake up there, that man,' mumbled the Corporal. 'Who's that man asleep there? What's your number?'

They all had their eyes closed now except Gunn, who sat with his hands clasped, rotating his thumbs, whose movements he forced himself to watch in order to prevent himself from ...

What? To his horror, he had a suspicion that if he looked anywhere but at his rotating thumbs he would see hordes of hairy brutes wandering about, all watching him with bloodshot eyes as they wandered about, floundering in the mud.

Around and around, his thumbs spun, round and round one another, while his head became heavier and heavier, a ball that spun round and round on his neck.

He breathed ever so gently, lest the brutes might hear him.

Darkness was coming, again hiding the horror of the battlefield within the shroud of its own eternal ugliness. But the gloom only increased Gunn's distorted vision.

The brutes kept springing up all round him, moving about, making strange gestures with their paws, calling on him to join them.

His countenance was assuming the expression of a brute and his body was becoming hard — so he thought — becoming possessed of superhuman strength.

Heavy steps approached. Gunn, thinking they were sounds made by the creatures of his hallucination, took no notice. Then he heard a bored voice say, 'What post is this?'

He looked up and saw Lieutenant Bull crouching above the hole. Gunn did not speak, being only faintly impressed and not at all intimidated by the appearance of the officer. The Corporal, on the other hand, at once sprang from his sleep and instinctively tried to bring his fists to his thighs in salute.

'Sir,' he said, 'No. 2 bombers.'

The officer's face was drawn and still more melancholy than on the previous night. Although he looked well nourished and almost quite clean, his countenance was even more repulsive that those of the soldiers because it contained the ghost of intelligence that had died of horror.

He still smelt of whisky and carried his club.

Shaw and Reilly, as soon as they heard his voice, began to dig. Lamont and McDonald still slept. The officer said, 'Where are the others?'

'Dead, sir,' said the Corporal.

'I see,' said the officer. 'Why are those men asleep?'

He stepped into the hole and whacked the sleepers with his club, saying, 'Wake up! Wake up! You can't sleep here. You mustn't let your men go to sleep, Corporal. Take their names.'

'Sir,' said the Corporal in a trembling voice. 'What's your number, McDonald?'

McDonald, rubbing his eyes, chattered, 'No. 8637 Private Jeremiah McDonald. I lost my — eh — eh ... rations, sir, when ...'

'You are to move on, Corporal,' said the officer, 'and occupy ...'

'Sir,' said the Corporal.

The officer, without finishing his sentence, leant on his elbows and looked out towards the enemy. He lay beside Gunn, who was now grinning, twitching his lips and sniffing. A maniacal joy had now taken possession of Gunn.

'Any definite idea where that fire was coming from?' said the officer.

'Yes, sir,' said the Corporal, lying down beside him and pointing. 'Just about there. Can't be far, as they got the range with rifle grenades.'

'Hah!' said the officer. 'It's a machine-gun nest. We must try and capture them. You'll probably ... later ... go ... just about there, I should think. Probably just the one lot. They keep moving about under cover of that ... You're to come along. Follow me.'

They picked up their tools and their weapons. They followed the officer, leaving the hole which they had dug with such trouble and where No. 11145 Private Simon Jennings, formerly an officer in the Army Service Corps, received a mortal wound in the right forearm.

Now it was freezing. The earth's surface had already begun to harden. There was dead silence on the battle front. Stooping, they walked about three hundred yards, until they came to a large shell hole, shaped like the sole of a shoe. The officer pointed at the hole with his stick.

'Here you are,' he said. 'Occupy this. Corporal Wallace is on your right, over there. If anything happens, get in touch with him. Later ... I'll let you know ... You'll send a man for rations ... later ... you'll be warned. Good luck in the meantime. We may have to send you out to capture ...'

Again he drifted away into the gloom.

The men stepped down into the hole and gaped at it. The narrow end of it, the heel of the shoe, was a puddle. The wide part, the thick of the sole, was littered with refuse. It had been occupied recently by the enemy.

'Come on, lads,' said the Corporal. 'Dig in.'

Gunn burst out laughing. All looked at Gunn. They could barely see him in the dusk. Now it was almost night. They could only see his figure outlined against the horizon. His head was thrust forward. His shoulders were hunched. He was looking into the distance, laughing. They were so exhausted that they did not comprehend the meaning of his laughter. They themselves were almost insane. But his insane laughter goaded them into an outburst of hysteria.

'What are you laughing at, you fool?' said the Corporal.

Then Reilly, the old soldier, burst out laughing, and cried, 'Take his number, Corporal.'

'I have an awful pain in my guts,' said Lamont, dropping his rifle to the bottom of the hole.

'I'll give you a worse pain, Lamont,' said the Corporal, 'if you laugh like that again.'

'I didn't laugh,' said Lamont.

'Well! Dig, then,' said the Corporal, almost in a scream, although his voice was scarcely audible. 'Dig! I say!'

'What'll we dig?' cried Shaw, striking the side of the hole with a pick. 'It's as hard as iron. Hear it ring as on an anvil.'

'God!' said McDonald. 'We'll freeze here. Oh! Christ! What cold! Oh! My bloody bones!'

'We'll never come back,' said Reilly. 'Not one of us.'

'Dig,' said the Corporal.

Gunn laughed again, and seizing the pick which Shaw had dropped, he hacked at the side of the hole.

Then stupidly, moving their limbs like figures in a dance, with their eyes almost closed, they began to prod the sides of the hole. The earth rang, as if jeering at their impotent blows.

Then the Corporal cried out, 'Blast it! I'm fed up. Sit down, lads, and have a smoke. It's no bloody use. Look at this hole. We go from bad to worse. No dug-out. Nowhere to drum up. Nothing. Then they expect us to go out on a bombing raid and capture some — Jerries.'

He sat down and folded his arms. They all sat down. The Corporal almost immediately called out angrily, 'Hey! Someone has to go on sentry. It's your turn, Gunn.'

'I've just been on sentry,' said Gunn.

'Then it's your turn, McDonald.'

McDonald grumbled. He got up and laid his rifle over the edge of the hole.

The Corporal lit a cigarette.

'Nobody else has a smoke, Corporal,' said Reilly. 'How about dishing us out one each, from that packet, till the rations come up?'

'Who said there were going to be cigarettes in the rations?' said the Corporal. 'There might be no rations.'

114

'The officer said there would,' said McDonald. 'I'll do myself in if there are no rations.'

'All right, Corporal,' said Reilly. 'Keep your fags.'

'Here they are,' said the Corporal, with an oath.

He struck Reilly on the face with the packet.

'Don't do that again,' said Reilly, clutching his rifle. He was panting.

Gunn, grinning, reached over and caught the packet. The Corporal kicked Gunn on the hand.

'Leave that alone,' he growled. 'You'll get none, you bastard.'

Gunn moved back slowly, seized his rifle, clubbed it and then rose, very slowly, breathing loudly.

'Who's a bastard?' he growled.

Shaw jumped up and stood between them.

'Fall in two men,' gasped the Corporal, struggling to his feet.

'Do you know what you're doing, Gunn?' cried Shaw.

Still gripping his rifle by the barrel, Gunn stepped back and crouched with his back to the side of the hole, beside Lamont, watching the Corporal like an animal at bay.

'Stay close to me, matey,' he whispered.

'He's going to attack us,' cried McDonald.

Shaw and Reilly held down the Corporal, who was trying to unfix his bayonet, in order to use it as a dagger.

'Keep your hair on,' they kept saying.

McDonald pointed his bayonet at Gunn.

'Don't move,' he cried, 'or I'll stab you in the guts.'

'I'm not interfering with you,' said Gunn. 'Turn away that bayonet.'

At that moment a shell burst to the rear, quite a distance away. They all ducked, although there was no danger. A machine-gun began to fire still further away. Somebody called out, 'Bombers.'

'Here,' said Reilly, standing up. 'Who's that?'

A man ran towards the hole and plunged down into it. He was one of Corporal Wallace's men.

'One of your men for rations,' he said, panting.

'Eh? What's that? Rations?'

Food!

Like a wild dog, who, when he sees a strip of raw beef in an intruder's hand, covers his snarling teeth, thrusts forth his lolling tongue and comes forward with limp tail, smelling, so these men, who had a moment before been snarling at one another like madmen, became transformed at the thought of food. Their faces shone with joy. They uttered excited cries. They gathered around the Lewis gunner, questioning him.

He knew nothing, being as excited as they were and just as stupefied by mud, rain, cold, lice, hunger, terror and long, aimless wandering from hole to hole.

'Hurry up!' he said in answer to their questions. 'One of you come along.'

'I'll go! Corporal,' said McDonald.

'Better send me, Corporal,' said Reilly.

'You go, Shaw,' said the Corporal.

Shaw at once unfixed his bayonet and followed the Lewis gunner out of the hole. They called after him, urging him to hurry. The Corporal rubbed his hands.

'There are only six of us,' he said, 'for nine men's rations. There might be two men to a loaf. I know there's bread.'

'I don't care what there is,' said Reilly, 'provided there are fags.'

They grew silent, thinking of food.

Gunn's face now began to work feverishly. The thought of food had disturbed his hatred of the Corporal. It had weakened him, relaxing his muscles, causing a void in his stomach. He could not resist wanting to fawn on the enemy who held the strip of beef.

'Say, Corporal,' he said, 'can't you give a bloke a chance?'

'Eh?' said the Corporal.

There was a heavy silence in the hole. They all peered at Gunn, again aware that they had with them a man who seemed to be going mad.

'What have you against me?' continued Gunn.

Even though he wanted to fawn, his voice was arrogant. The Corporal did not reply, being in doubt as to what he should say. As it were, he had at last been stripped of his Corporal's stripes and of his authority by exhaustion. He faced Gunn now as man to man and was silent because he was an inferior man. It was a struggle between two brutes, and Gunn was the superior brute.

Lamont tapped Gunn's arm and tried to whisper something, but Gunn roughly brushed the youth aside.

'I leave it to any of the men here,' said Gunn. 'Haven't I always done my share of soldiering, Reilly?'

'Always found you a good mate,' said Reilly.

'I've nothing against you,' said the Corporal. 'I'm responsible for discipline in this section, though.'

'When you got wounded at Loos,' said Gunn, 'I carried you under heavy fire back to the dressing station. You were whining like a dog. You had only a bloody scratch. First thing you did when you came out of dock was to get me No. 1. I was tied to a bloody tree for seven days.'

'You broke camp and got into a fight with a lot of Froggies in an *estaminet*,' said the Corporal. 'You sold your boots for Vin Blanc.'

'You always had your knife in me,' said Gunn. 'Every time I did you a good turn you hated me all the more for it. You might be drowned now with Appleby only for me. You have your knife in my chum because he won't give you half his parcels. It is no damn good. It seems I won't be let soldier in this mob. I ain't the sort of a bloke that gets sour over nothing. I was doing field punishment No. 1 when I got the D.C.M., on the canal bank for capturing six of a Fritzy raiding party single-handed. I'll fight my share with any man in this mob. I've always done my bit. I was one of four out of the whole company that finished the march to Arras standing up. Why can't I be let alone?'

'I ain't got nothing against you,' the Corporal repeated.

Reilly, deeply moved by Gunn's speech, came over and struck Gunn on the back.

'Forget it, mate,' he said. 'See?'

'Reilly,' said Gunn, 'you're the only bloody soldier in this mob. I hope you get out of it.'

'That doesn't worry me,' said Reilly. 'I know I'm for it, sooner or later. I know I'm unlucky. I've been out since the first shot was fired in 1914 without a scratch. So I know I'll get mine shortly. But that doesn't worry me. I've drunk a nice lot of beer in my time. Had a good few tidy wenches. Something to look back on when I'm dead. But look at it this way. Every good soldier has his grouse, but he never lets it get hold of him.'

'To hell with being a good soldier,' said Gunn. 'A good soldier means one thing to you and me, but it means another thing to THEM. To you and me it means a MAN. To them it means a —— clod.'

'I've been through it, mate,' said Reilly. 'You needn't tell me. The only clink I ain't copped is the Tower. The best place to look for a good soldier is tied to the wheel of the cookhouse cart. A bloke has got to stick it.'

'That's all right, mate,' said Gunn. 'Don't worry. They'll never have to crime me again.'

'That's the ticket, Gunn,' said the Corporal in a friendly tone. 'You muck in with me. I muck in with you. Savvy?'

'Why are they so friendly towards me?' thought Gunn. 'They are treating me as if I were a child.'

Now he could not remember that there had been anything the matter with him all day, or that he had done, or said, or thought, or seen, anything odd or irregular. He was greatly worried by the soothing manner of Reilly, who was always so cynical and utterly devoid of feeling. He was especially worried by the Corporal's friendly tone.

Now the four men in the post seemed to have become entirely remote and alien to him; just as when a man is falling asleep under the influence of ether, he hears the voices of the doctors and the nurse as voices heard from afar, entirely inhuman.

This was a great torture, from which he could not save himself. He felt bound hand and foot by it. He tried to talk to Lamont; but Lamont answered him in the same tone as the others.

119

The others had now become very quiet. They were whispering to one another. Why were they whispering so quietly? He must talk to them.

'I say, lads,' he said.

'What?' said Reilly.

He could not remember what he wanted to say for nearly a minute. Then he burst forth, 'I know now who's running this show. Up here ye want it.' He tapped his forehead. Then he shuddered and glanced around him furtively, ashamed of what he had said. 'Why don't they let us fight?' he cried. 'It's this crawling around in the — mud that's killing us.'

Nobody answered him. Reilly tipped the Corporal and then walked over to the narrow end of the hole. He began to void his bladder. The Corporal followed, leaned up against the side of the hole and began also to void his bladder.

'Better send him back,' said Reilly. 'He's going mad.'

'Eh?' said the Corporal. 'Do you think so?'

He himself was quite sure that Gunn was mad, and he had been thinking for the past few minutes that Gunn should be sent back at once. But now, on being advised by Reilly to let Gunn go back, his hatred of Gunn made him oppose the idea.

He said to himself, 'He won't escape me that way.'

'He's only malingering,' he whispered. 'He and the kid have it made up between them. He knows he's for it when he gets back for insubordination in the line, so he's gamming on mad. That's all.'

'That may be so,' said Reilly, 'but I doubt it. I think he's really going bugs. You remember '53 Jones, that went daft on the canal. He killed two men before he could be knocked out. He started just that way. He was in the same dug-out as me. Fritz shelled us for twelve hours without a break. He began the same sort of gibberish about the war and everything. I'd send him back, Corporal.'

The Corporal looked towards Gunn, and saw Gunn looking towards him.

'He'll go back when I go back,' he said, 'and not before. I'm not afraid of him.'

'In that case,' said Reilly, shrugging his shoulders, 'none of us'll ever go back. I can see it coming.'

'Talking about me?' cried Gunn, angrily.

They walked back.

'It's all right,' said Gunn. 'I can guess what you were saying.'

'I think I'm poisoned,' said McDonald. 'I have an awful pain in my guts. I ate a piece of black Jerry bread I found here.'

'There are worse deaths,' said Reilly, casually. 'You'll die soon anyway, one way or another. I saw a fellow die of eating a feed of dirty straw.'

'Why don't they let us fight?' cried Gunn.

'You'll soon get a bellyful of fighting,' said the Corporal.

'When I went on leave,' said McDonald, 'I said to myself I'd spend all day and all night eating. But ye can't eat there either. Not enough.'

'That's right,' cried Gunn, eagerly. 'You can't get away from it. They've got you everywhere, in London as well as here. They've got everybody, us, Jerries, Froggies, the lousy Russians and those dirty little Belgians. You'll parade everywhere as well as here, full marching order, housewife and hold-all complete. Hear that, Louis. Don't hide your bloody head. Face it, kid. You got to fight them. As Reilly says, we're all for it. Let's have it then and be done with it.'

A cold sweat was breaking out all over his body. Red stars began to dance before his eyes. Reilly tipped the Corporal. The Corporal growled.

'You can't work it that way, Gunn,' he said. 'Why not try something cleverer than that? Can't you work a trench foot?'

'Don't you worry, Corporal,' said Gunn, tapping his forehead. 'Up here you want it. I've got it now.'

Reilly got to his feet and moved about restlessly.

'Jesus!' said McDonald. 'I think I have trench feet. It's freezing like hell. My guts are freezing too.'

'Go sick, quick,' said Reilly. 'Then I'll have your rations.'

'Christ!' said Gunn. 'A General! That's what I want. A bloody General. Why don't Generals come into the front line. Them are the blokes I want to talk to. I'll tell 'em something.'

They all looked at him again in silence. He now spoke in an exalted voice and although they could not see his face in the darkness, they could feel a strange force in his presence. Something alien and terrifying had taken possession of him.

'Something the matter with my kidneys,' said Reilly, again moving over to the puddle.

The icy ground now crackled under his feet.

'Don't worry, Reilly,' cried Gunn. 'You won't be long now.'

Lamont had not spoken or moved for half an hour. He

had surrendered to the cold and lay at the bottom of the hole, with his head fallen on his chest, rapidly losing consciousness. There was a smile on his lips and he was dreaming of his home.

There was now heavy firing on the left. The enemy was firing at the ration party. Several machine-guns were in action. Rifle grenades were bursting. But nobody in the hole took any notice of the firing. Their limbs moved continuously, jerking, twisting about. Their mouths and nostrils twitched. They kept getting to their feet and sitting down again; all except Lamont who sat very still. They could no longer speak.

When they touched one another by chance they started violently. The slightest noise in the hole excited them, the scraping of a boot on the icy earth, the rattle of a gun butt on a stone, a cough.

Now the sky was bright with stars. The enemy began to rake their post intermittently with machine-gunfire. Single shots rang out, like the popping of corks. In the distance there was a heavy roar, like a mountain river pouring through a gorge. On the far left, a corner of the sky was covered with a bright red arc of flame, above which rolling clouds of smoke rose in widening wreaths. Verey lights passed through the sky in beautiful curves and fell in streamers of fire. The earth shone with frost.

The night was very beautiful.

Chapter Ten

Suddenly they heard voices whispering to the rear of the hole, some distance away.

'There they are,' cried Reilly, eagerly. 'That's Shaw and Hurley with the rations. Whist! Listen.'

They crouched against the bank, listening. The voices were a mumble. The Corporal peered over the top. Although the night was quite bright, he could distinguish nothing moving over the dun back of the uneven earth. Here and there a pool of water gleamed, a coil of wire stood out, a stake, a sheet of zinc. In the distance there was a mound, running zig-zag: a trench. The earth was monotonously similar. All holes, water and débris. Dead. An unroofed tomb.

The whispering went on. It stopped at moments and then there were sounds of feet crawling over the hard earth. A Verey light was shot by the enemy. The Corporal bowed his head and lay still. The voices ceased. The air became as bright as by day while the streaming light fell beyond the hole. Then the light withered, hissing. Darkness returned. There was a rush of feet. A machine-gun began to rattle, the bullets speeding past the hole on the right.

'They've copped them,' whispered McDonald.

'Hush!'

The firing stopped. Then there was a rapid rush of feet going to the right. Then a body dropped to the earth, heavily. They could hear a clank of metal striking the frost-bound earth. The machine-gun again opened fire. Another Verey light came over. Brilliant light was followed by darkness. A terrible silence.

'That was Hurley running, away to the right,' whispered McDonald. 'Where's Shaw?'

Reilly swallowed his breath and muttered, 'I'm going out to look for him.'

'Wait a mo',' said the Corporal. 'Listen!'

They heard a groan.

'That's Shaw,' said Reilly. 'He's hit. I'm going ...'

'Wait,' said the Corporal. 'Here he comes. He's not hit.'

Peering, they saw Shaw, crawling along slowly, with a sack on his back. He was hauling himself on his belly, using his hands and one leg. The other leg dragged after him.

'He's hit!' cried Reilly, jumping up to the top of the hole.

'Down!' cried the Corporal.

Another Verey light came over. Reilly dropped to the ground. The glare of the light caught Shaw as he lay prone, like a snail, with his grub sack on his back. His steel hat had fallen back on his neck. The stocking cap which he wore beneath the hat covered half his skull. The front of his skull, above his forehead, shone baldly in the light.

The light had scarcely died down when the firing began again. In spite of that, Reilly jumped to his feet, ran to

Shaw and lay down beside him.

'Are you hit, '20?' he said.

'That you, '48?' whispered Shaw. 'Yes. Got it some-where in the leg. Hip, I think. Take these rations.'

Lying flat on the ground, Reilly took the sack. The machine-gun was still firing, trying to find them. Being old soldiers they lay so flat on the ground that their bodies hardly broke the surface, even though they lay in an exposed place.

'I'll pull you along,' said Reilly, 'when this stops.'

Shaw ground his teeth. Then he whispered, 'You go on. I'll make my way back. I think I got another one some-where.'

'Where?'

'I don't know. Somewhere in the back. I think I'm warned for parade the other side. I just wanted to bring up the rations.'

Reilly swore at the enemy machine-gunner in a long and obscene oath. His voice was broken. The other casu-alties meant little to him. They were only war soldiers. But Shaw was an old soldier, one of the 'regiment', part of his life; joined to him in that close brotherhood which is more binding even than blood relationship, the comrade-ship of men who are bound by oath and ancient traditions to give their whole lives to the service of a regiment.

Lying there together on the ground, while the machine hissed at them, as if in conscious hatred, the two men clasped hands, and were silent for a few moments; and without thinking of it actually, the consciousness of their past associations welled gloriously through their beings in a wave of romantic splendour; all the pride of a soldier's life, the rattle of drums, the thunderous music of brass instruments, the applause of multitudes as the disciplined companies march past with a swaying rhythm, the singing in taverns of war songs; battles, and after them, the parade of the survivors before the battalion commander, who, astride his horse, harangues his men in a voice that is harsh with pride and sorrow for the dead; all the queer, foolish romance of a soldier's life that only a professional soldier can understand.

Shaw made no complaint. Neither did he cry out at his wounds, but calmly accepted them as part of his duty. And he had crawled three hundred yards, badly wounded, with the rations, without even thinking that he was doing anything brave or worthy of praise. He was merely obeying an order. His voice was steady. Only by the grinding of his teeth did he give any sign of the torture he was suffering.

It is such men who give glory to the foul horror of war.

'Half a mo',' said Reilly. 'I'll just take the rations over and then I'll ...'

'Don't worry, '48,' said Shaw. 'Take the rations. I'll get back.'

'No. Don't stir. Are you bleeding much?'

'Don't worry, '48,' said Shaw. 'Go on with the rations. I'm finished soldiering.'

Reilly picked up the sack and plunged headlong towards the hole. He threw himself down into it. They began to question him excitedly, but he waved his hands and muttered, 'Shaw's wounded out there, Corporal. Got any ...?'

They hurriedly procured field dressings. He dashed

out again, pursued by bullets. He found that Shaw had crawled back about ten yards and now lay with his head and chest in a small hole, while the remainder of his body stuck up on level ground. Reilly slid into the hole, raised the head and looked at the face. Shaw's lips were moving but his eyes were fixed.

'Say, mate,' said Reilly.

Shaw answered by vomiting a quantity of blood with a horrid sound. Then he began to shudder. Reilly laid down the head quietly. He also shuddered. Then he began to mutter, 'It ain't right. Something wrong here. We'll all be wiped out. Your time has come, '48 Reilly. You're for it, lad.'

He began to twist the ends of his moustache and gazed at Shaw's dead body, no longer feeling any emotion or sympathy. Shaw, the old soldier, had ceased to be. That thing was only a corpse. He shook his head and shuddered to banish a vague thought that had crawled into his mind. It was a doubt as to the wisdom of his superiors, a doubt as to the use of war. He brushed it aside and became thoughtless, without sympathy for the dead, without emotion as regarded his own future. He began to grumble in a soldierly manner about the cold.

He was getting to his feet to go back and report Shaw's death to the Corporal, when he heard sounds of a man approaching from the right. He hailed the sounds. A voice answered, saying, 'Corporal Wallace. Who are you?'

Reilly answered. The Corporal crawled over.

'Who's that?' he whispered, nodding towards Shaw's corpse.

Reilly answered. Corporal Wallace's strained expression only for a moment showed signs of being concerned with the death of Shaw, by a twitching of the nostrils. Then he looked sharply at Reilly and said, 'Tell Corporal Williams to come along with me. Where's your post? You blokes are going over on a raid.'

'Post's over there,' said Reilly. 'It's only a couple of yards.'

'I've got to get back to my post,' said Corporal Wallace. 'Tell him to come along. See? It's over there.'

He pointed. Then he crawled away to the right. Reilly crawled off to the front. They crawled in different directions from the corpse of Shaw, which had ceased to crawl and lay idle in death.

When Reilly got back, they had already opened the sack and begun to share the rations.

'Shaw's dead,' said Reilly.

'There's no bread and no fags,' said McDonald.

'Is he dead?' said the Corporal.

'You're to go over to Corporal Wallace's post,' said Reilly. 'There's going to be a raid. We're for it.'

The Corporal jumped up. 'Only lousy biscuits,' he said. 'God! That's tough about Shaw. I've only four men now and look at them.'

'Warn the stretcher-bearers,' said Reilly. 'We can't leave him lying out there.'

'Whereabouts is Wallace?'

Reilly pointed, showing him the direction.

'You take charge here,' said the Corporal, leaving the hole. 'Don't let anybody touch the rations.'

He crawled out under heavy fire and twisted himself along the ground. Gunn looked after him and swore under his breath. Reilly looked at Gunn and suddenly got very angry with the fellow.

'I'm in charge here now, Bill,' he said. 'Cut it out.'

'What?' said Gunn.

'Put a sock in it,' said Reilly. 'A Corporal is a Corporal and what's more he's a good soldier, even if he has his faults.'

Gunn stared at Reilly and then pointed to the huddled figure of Lamont.

'Look at my mate,' he whispered, fiercely.

Reilly looked. Lamont sat very still with his arms folded and his head on his chest.

'Kid should have been ...' began Reilly. Then he added, 'What's the matter with him?'

'You go and touch him,' said Gunn. 'See? Go and touch him. He doesn't know.'

'Who doesn't know?'

'The Corporal.'

Reilly stepped back and looked at McDonald and saw the latter putting a tin of bully beef into his haversack.

'What are you doing with those rations?'

'Aren't they divided?' said McDonald. 'I'm replacing my ...'

'You go and touch him,' said Gunn, crouching towards Reilly.

There was a note of malignant joy in Gunn's voice. Reilly began to tremble. Then he shook himself and went over to Lamont.

'Hey, lad,' he whispered.

'He won't hear you,' said Gunn, going on one knee. 'Touch him, though. Touch his face. Then you'll see. I didn't want to draw attention to him while the Corporal was here. See? He's better that way. Look at the smile on his face. He was thinking of her. God only knows how he did it or where he is now. But he's not here. I knew he had a plan, but I thought it was something else. He never said a word. He tipped my arm there about an hour ago, but I didn't spot anything. See?'

'Hey! Lad,' said Reilly. 'Good Christ! Is he ...?'

'See that?' said Gunn excitedly. 'Not a move. He can't be touched. They can shout as much as they like but they can't waken him. Fire a shot past his ear now to see can you waken him.'

'Good Christ!' said Reilly, kneeling beside the boy and putting his ear to his chest.

'What's up?' said McDonald, coming over.

'You touch him, then,' said Gunn arrogantly to McDonald. 'Then you'll see. They terrified the life out of him. That's it. It's not the cold that did it. It's they did it.'

'He's stone cold,' said Reilly. 'Good God! That's five.'

'You can't touch him, though,' said Gunn, in an exalted voice. 'She wrote to me and said I was to look after him, not to let anybody touch him. See? Nobody has laid a hand on him. He just sat down there and went to sleep.'

McDonald went back to the rations and picked up a biscuit which he began to chew.

'Leave those rations alone,' cried Reilly.

Gunn folded his arms and continued to talk to rapidly. Reilly went over, took the biscuit from McDonald and growled, 'I'm in charge here. Understand that?'

McDonald munched the piece of biscuit he had in his mouth and mumbled, 'Is he dead?'

'Every man has got his rights,' said Gunn. 'And any

man that takes his rights from another man deserves to die. But who took them? A million men can't be killed by one man. But one man can. But may God, if there is a God, curse and burn whoever is responsible for the pain in my head.'

Then he sat down beside Lamont and said, 'Hey! Reilly!'

'What do you want?' said Reilly.

'You can't touch him,' said Gunn.

'Where the hell is the Corporal?' said Reilly.

The three of them were now sitting at a distance, one from the other.

McDonald's teeth began to chatter. 'Oh! My bones!' he mumbled. 'Oh! My bloody bones!'

Chapter Eleven

The Corporal came back. As soon as he entered the hole, he called out, 'Reilly, you stay here. McDonald, Gunn and Lamont are coming with me. We're going out on a raid. Get ready, lads.'

'Aw! Aw! Aw!' cried McDonald. 'What about the rations? Is there going to be nothing in our bellies when we die?'

'Corporal,' whispered Reilly. 'Lamont is ...'

'He can't touch him now,' said Gunn.

'What?' said the Corporal, excitedly. 'What about Lamont? Asleep again? Hey! You!' He dashed over to Lamont and seized him.

'You can't touch him,' cried Gunn, exultantly.

'Christ!' said the Corporal, dropping Lamont. 'He's stiff.'

'Five gone now,' said Reilly in a gloomy voice. 'There's something queer about it. I say, Corporal. Half a mo'.'

'What?' cried the Corporal. 'What do you want? No time now. Get ready. Get those bombs ready. As soon as the Lewis gun opens fire ... What do you want?'

Reilly drew him aside and whispered in his ear, 'Let Gunn stay here. I'll go. You can't ...'

'You're detailed, blast it,' cried the Corporal.

'But don't you see ...'

'You stay here. Your orders are ...'

Gunn knelt beside Lamont and began to pray with his hands clasped. Then he got to his feet and cried, 'Come on now. I'm ready.'

Soon the Lewis gun opened fire.

'Up,' said the Corporal.

They swung out of the hole all together, ran and dropped. Reilly stretched himself and lay flat against the side of the hole with his rifle pointed towards the enemy.

'No bloody fags,' he said. 'Nothing.'

Chapter Twelve

After their first run they began to crawl, the Corporal in front, Gunn behind him on the right, McDonald on the left. Gunn's eyes were fixed on the Corporal's back.

Gunn was now completely unconscious of his environment. His mind was entirely concentrated on the Corporal. As he crawled, a loud voice kept crying out within him, uttering one word: 'Now.' The word appeared before his eyes like an electric sign, in varying colours, sometimes composed of enormous letters, sometimes quite tiny. The letters were made of fire and he thought he belched them from a furnace within himself. The interior of his body appeared to be full of monstrous sound, the roaring of flames. There was also, in some remote part of his body, very distant and faint, a chorus of birds, of many species, singing in beautiful harmony. The whole world had changed into sound. The sounds of his feet, touching the frosty earth, were magnified, and, as he crawled, his body seemed to rise and fall like a boat tossed from the crests of tall waves down into wave troughs and up again. The earth rolled like a

sea, undulating. The air rushed past his ears with a
buzzing tumult.

Now he was aware that a vast multitude of brutes
was crawling with him, tracking the Corporal. He no
longer feared the brutes, but felt akin to them and
savagely proud of their hairy bodies and of their smell,
and of their snorting breath. On all sides they rose in
myriads, some enormous, some as small as ferrets,
some with monstrous bellies, some as thin as snakes;
all with protruding fangs and eyes that belched fire.
All made the same sounds as they moved, a pattering of
furred paws, like the pattering of heavy raindrops on a
lake.

The Corporal halted, listened with his ear to the
ground and made a sign with his hand. Gunn and
McDonald halted. Then the Corporal said 'up', jumped to
his feet and ran forward with a bomb in his hand. They
followed him.

Gunn stumbled, fell, rose again and ran on.

The Corporal and McDonald jumped down into a
hole, out of sight. Then the word, 'Now,' appearing
before Gunn's eyes, expanded and burst with a crash.
The sounds ceased. The flames were extinguished. For a
moment he felt terribly cold. Then he growled. Instead
of following the Corporal and McDonald into their hole,
he rushed aside and dropped into another hole. He was
panting loudly. He took out a bomb from his bag and
pulled the pin. He waited, listening. The Corporal and
McDonald were about eight yards away in the other
hole.

'They're gone,' said the Corporal. 'See?'

'What are we to do now?' said McDonald.

'Hush!' said the Corporal. 'Listen. They're gone back there. See? Where's Gunn?'

Then Gunn stood up in his hole and growled, 'Here I am.'

He hurled the bomb into their hole.

'Christ!'

It struck McDonald in the face. He fell backwards. The bomb rolled to the ground beside him. The Corporal threw himself out of the hole and lay flat. The bomb burst, shattering McDonald's head to a pulp, sending his steel hat flying into the air.

'There he is now,' cried Gunn, jumping out of his hole.

The Corporal raised his head, saw Gunn and then jumped to his feet. The two men rushed at one another. The Corporal had his bayoneted rifle pointed. Gunn carried his rifle like a club, holding it by the barrel. He swung his weapon when he came near. The Corporal put up his weapon to ward off the blow. His rifle was knocked from his hands. He stumbled and fell. Gunn hurtled forward, tripped over the Corporal's body and fell a few yards away, dropping his rifle.

They both got to their feet at the same time. The Corporal stooped for his rifle, but before he could catch it, Gunn was on top of him. They fell to the ground and grappled with one another. They fought in silence, breathing heavily, tossing about on the ground, rolling over and over, butting with their heads, kicking and biting like animals. In spite of Gunn's great size and his strength, he could not overcome the Corporal, who twisted like an eel. It was impossible to hold him.

Then, suddenly, Gunn gathered himself together and threw his whole weight on the Corporal, pinning him to the ground. The Corporal began to gnash his teeth.

'Now,' cried Gunn, and again the word appeared before his eyes in letters of fire.

Then with his chest pressed against the Corporal's writhing body, he slowly sought the throat, found it and enlaced it with his fingers and pressed fiercely. The Corporal began to go limp. Then he lay still.

Gunn clutched the throat for a long time after the Corporal had become still. Then, uttering queer sounds, he began to mangle the body with his bare hands.

Now he was really an animal, brutish, with dilated eyes, with his face bloody.

Suddenly he got up, looked about him furtively and ran off, crouching. He set out in the direction of the enemy, moving at a jog trot. Then he changed direction and began to trot about in a zig-zag course, mumbling.

They began to fire at him from somewhere. Hearing the shots he halted and uttered a queer cry, like the bellow of an animal. Then he ran on bellowing.

A bullet struck him. He fell and then jumped up at once. He waved his arms about his head and ran on, bellowing.

He was running around in a circle.

Then they turned a machine-gun on him and brought him down.

Riddled with bullets, he died, bellowing and clawing the earth.

Later, Reilly came with two Lewis gunners to look for the raiding party. When they examined Gunn they found his face and hands covered with the Corporal's gore.

Next day, the battalion was relieved.

No. 4048 Private Daniel Reilly was the only one of Corporal Williams' section who came back alive.

THE END

BY THE SAME AUTHOR

Mr. Gilhooley

'Mr. Laurence Gilhooley emerged from The Bailey
restaurant in Duke Street, Dublin. He was slightly drunk,
having eaten a heavy dinner and finished two bottles of
red wine. He stood in front of the door, swaying gently.
His eyes were half closed. His head was thrust
backwards. He looked from side to side, wondering
whither he was going to turn for his night's amusement.'

'*Mr Gilhooley* reads like a Dickens novel written by Sartre.'
Fintan O'Toole

Forty-nine-year-old Mr Gilhooley is living two lives:
the one drinking in the pubs of Dublin, the other
desperate and lonely, longing for love. A chance
encounter with the innocent yet destructive Nelly starts a
chain of compelling, dark and menacing events.

This is the underworld of 1920s Dublin.
Death, violence, sex, religion and love intertwine
in this visually rich and passionate tragi-comedy.

ISBN 0-86327-641-5

A Tourist's Guide to Ireland

From Ireland's master storyteller comes what appears to
be a simple tourist guide; but underneath this harmless
surface lies a scathing satire on Irish society. No aspect of
newly-independent Ireland is safe from his attack.

The Civil War was absurd and futile; the attempt to revive
the Irish language is a political gimmick; the politicians,
more concerned with Ireland's soul than with its body, are
on the verge of turning the country into a 'clerical
kingdom'; the priests, concerned only with power, use
religion to enslave the people and oppose any writing
that questions their blinkered beliefs; and the peasants,
Ireland's only hope, must rid themselves of these
parasites before they can become 'civilised citizens'.

A vivid, controversial insight into life
in the Ireland of the 1930s —
as powerful and challenging today as it was 60 years ago.

ISBN 0-86327-589-3

Famine

'The author's skill as a storyteller is at times breathtaking.
This is a most rewarding novel.'
Publishers Weekly

Set in the period of the Great Famine of the 1840s,
Famine is the story of three generations
of the Kilmartin family.
It is a masterly historical novel,
rich in language, character and plot,
a panoramic story of passion, tragedy and resilience.

'O'Flaherty is the most heroic of Irish novelists, the one
who has always tackled big themes, and in one case, in
this great novel, succeeded in writing something
imperishable ... Mary Kilmartin has been singled out by
two generations of critics as one of the great creations of
modern literature. And so she is.'
John Broderick, **Irish Times**

'I gladly accept one of the claims on the dustjacket of this
novel: "A major achievement — a masterpiece" ...
It is the kind of truth only a major writer of fiction
is capable of portraying.'
Anthony Burgess, **Irish Press**

ISBN 0-86327-043-3

Short Stories
The Pedlar's Revenge

'The finest Irish writer of his generation.'
John Banville, **Irish Times**

'This collection is a gallery of human emotions, embracing
a clutch of huge eccentrics, sweet and sour remembrances
of distant youth and vivid portraits of rural Ireland ...
A worthy representation of an unflinching lyric writer.'
The Sunday Times

'This valuable collection displays O'Flaherty's amazing
range, from a love idyll between a wild drake and a
domestic duck to the unspeakable comedy of the
appalling Patsa delivering the contents of his golden belly
under the influence of a cataclysmic purge, from the
burning of young love in that splendid story "The Caress"
to the rheumy old man sitting by the roadside and failing
to recognise, in the old woman who pauses in passing,
the love of his youth.'
Benedict Kiely

ISBN 0-86327-536-2

All books available from:
WOLFHOUND PRESS
68 Mountjoy Square
Dublin 1
Tel: (+353 1) 874 0354   Fax: (+353 1) 872 0207